"All right," A
you? And wh

"My name is Ho
reaching into her bag for a business card. "See? All The Trimmings. We do professional decorating and event planning for the Christmas holidays. I was hired to give your son his Christmas wish. I'm to work for you through to Christmas Day."

"Hired by whom?"

"I'm afraid I can't say. My contract forbids it."

"What is this? Charity? Or some busybody's idea of generosity?"

"No!" Holly assured him. "Not at all." She reached in her coat pocket and took out Eric's letter to Santa. "Maybe you should read this," she said, reaching out to touch his arm. The instant she grazed his skin a frisson of electricity suddenly shot through her fingers.

Dear Reader

Another holiday season is here, and since I finished all my shopping last summer (I wish!), I decided to add my devoted readers to this year's Christmas list. But what do I get the reader who has everything? Nothing I found seemed right, especially with so many tastes to take into account.

In the end I found a present I hope everyone will like—a brand-new story filled with romance, humour and Christmas cheer. UNEXPECTED ANGEL features all my favourite Christmas fantasies. So consider handsome hero Alex Marrin my gift to you.

Happy holidays!

Kate Hoffmann

P.S. I love to hear from my readers. You can write to me c/o Harlequin Books, 225 Duncan Mill Road, Don Mills, Ontario, M3B 3K9, Canada.

UNEXPECTED ANGEL

BY
KATE HOFFMANN

MILLS & BOON®

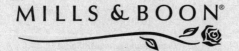

With special thanks to Faye and Charles McDaniels
who shared their love of horses with me
and gave me a peek inside the stable doors.

*First published in Great Britain 2002
Harlequin Mills & Boon Limited,
Eton House, 18-24 Paradise Road, Richmond, Surrey TW9 1SR*

© Peggy A. Hoffmann 2000

ISBN 0 263 82990 1

*Set in Times Roman 10½ on 12 pt.
01-1202-51661*

*Printed and bound in Spain
by Litografía Rosés, S.A., Barcelona*

1

IT WAS ALL EXACTLY as he'd remembered it. The little candy cane fence, the gingerbread cottage with the gumdrop roof, the elves dressed in red shoes with jingle bells around the ankles, and the tinsel-trimmed Christmas tree. Eric Marrin's heart skipped a beat and he clutched his mittened hands to still the tremble of excitement.

He peered around the chubby kid standing in front of him and caught a glimpse of the man he'd come to see, the man half the kids in Schuyler Falls, New York, had come to see this night. "Santa Claus," he murmured, his voice filled with awe.

As he stood in line waiting to take his turn on Santa's lap, he wondered whether his name was on the "nice" list. Eric made a quick mental review of the past twelve months.

Overall, it had been a pretty good year. Sure, there'd been the time he brought the garter snake into the house and then lost it. And the time he'd put his muddy shoes in the washing machine with his dad's best dress shirts. And the time he'd gotten caught down at the railroad tracks squashing pennies on the tracks with his best friends, Raymond and Kenny.

But in the whole seven and a half, almost eight, years of his life, he'd never done anything naughty on purpose—except maybe for today. Today, instead of going straight home from school, he'd hopped a city bus with

Raymond and jumped off right in front of Dalton's Department Store. Riding the city bus alone was strictly against his dad's rules and could result in punishment harsher than anything he'd seen in his life. But, technically, he hadn't been alone. Raymond had been with him. And the trip had been for a very good reason. Even his dad would have to see that.

Dalton's Department Store was considered by everyone in the second grade at Patrick Henry Elementary School as a shrine to Santa Claus. From the day after Thanksgiving until the hours leading up to Christmas Eve, children flocked though the shiny brass revolving doors and up the ancient escalator to the magical spot on the second floor where Santa and his minions reigned supreme.

Raymond claimed that a meeting with Dalton's Santa was much better than a visit to any other Santa in New York. Those others were all just "helpers," pretenders dressed up like the real Santa to help out during the Christmas rush. But this Santa was special. He had the power to make dreams come true. Kenny even knew a kid who'd gotten a trip to Florida just because his dad had lost his job right before Christmas.

Eric reached into his jacket pocket and pulled out the letter. He'd used his very best penmanship and sealed the note in a colorful green envelope. He'd even added some of his favorite smelly stickers to decorate the outside, just to make sure the letter stood out from all the others. For this was the most important letter he'd ever written and he'd stop at nothing to make sure it got into Santa's hands.

He watched as a little girl in a blue wool coat slipped her own letter into the ornate mailbox outside the Candy Cane Gate. She'd sealed it in a plain white envelope, addressed in sloppy crayon. Eric smiled. Surely her letter would be passed over for his. He closed his eyes and rubbed the lucky penny he always kept in his pocket. "Don't mess up," he murmured to himself. "Just don't mess up."

The line moved forward and Eric shoved the letter deeper into his pocket. First, he'd plead his case with Santa, and if the opportunity presented itself, he'd slip the letter into Santa's pocket. He could imagine the jolly old man sitting down at dinner that night and tucking his glasses into his pocket. He'd discover the letter and read it immediately.

Eric frowned. If he really wanted to do the job right, he'd come down every night after school with a new letter each time. Santa would have to see how important this was to him and grant his wish. Maybe they'd even become best friends and he'd invite Eric over to play at the North Pole. And he could bring Santa to school for show and tell! That old sourpuss, Eleanor Winchell, would be so jealous she'd have a cow.

Of course, Eleanor had read her letter to Santa out loud in front of Miss Green's class, a long recitation of all the toys she'd need to have a satisfying Christmas, the pretty dresses she'd require. She'd also informed the class that she planned to be the very first in line to give her letter to Santa once the Gingerbread Cottage opened for business at Dalton's.

Secretly, Eric hoped that Eleanor's letter would get lost in the shuffle, and that she'd fall through the ice on the Hudson River and she'd be swept downstream to torment some other kids at a grade school in faraway New York City. She was greedy and nasty and mean and if Santa couldn't see that from her letter, then he didn't deserve to drive a magic sleigh! Eric's wish for Christmas didn't include a single request for toys. And his Christmas wish was anything but selfish; it was as much for his dad as it was for himself.

Two years had passed since Eric's mom had walked out. He'd been five, almost six, years old and Christmas had been right around the corner. The stockings were hung and the tree decorated and then she'd left. And everything had turned sad after that.

The first Christmas without her had been hard, mostly because he thought she'd be coming back. But last Christmas had been even worse. His dad hadn't bothered to get a tree or hang the wreath on the door. Instead they'd left Thurston, their black lab, in a kennel, and flown to Colorado for skiing. The Christmas presents hadn't even been wrapped and Eric suspected Santa had passed them right by because their condo had a fake fireplace with a really skinny chimney.

"Hey, kid. You're next."

Eric snapped his head up and blinked. A pretty elf, dressed in a puffy red polka-dot jacket and baggy green tights, stood at the gate and motioned him closer with an impatient expression. Her name tag said Twinkie and he hurried up to her, his heart pounding. He was so nervous he could barely remember what he wanted to say.

"So," Twinkie said, "what are you going to ask for?"

Eric gave the elf a suspicious glance. "I think that's between me and Santa," he replied.

The elf chuckled. "Ah, the old Santa-kid confidentiality agreement."

Eric scowled. "Huh?"

Twinkie sighed and rolled her eyes. "Never mind."

He shifted back and forth between his feet, then forced a smile at the elf. "Do you know him pretty well?"

Twinkie shrugged. "As well as any elf," she said.

"Maybe you could give me some tips." He opened his

pocket and showed her the envelope, making sure that she saw his name scrawled in the upper left corner. If Santa didn't remember who he was, he'd be sure Twinkie did. "I really need him to read my letter. It's very, very, *very* important." He pulled a bright blue Gobstopper out of his other pocket. "Do you think if I gave him—"

She studied the envelope. "Well, Eric Marrin, I can tell you this. The big guy doesn't accept bribes."

"But, I—"

"You're up, kid," Twinkie said, pushing him forward, then quickly turning to the next person in line. Eric approached slowly, reviewing all he planned to say. Then he crawled up on Santa's lap and drew a steadying breath.

The smell of peppermint and pipe tobacco clung to his big red coat and tickled Eric's nose. His lap was broad and his belly soft as a feather pillow and Eric leaned closer and looked up into the jolly old man's eyes. Unlike the elf, Eric could see that Santa was patient and kind. "Are you really him?" he asked. Some of the kids at school claimed that Santa wasn't real, but this guy sure looked real.

Santa chuckled, his beard quivering in merriment. "That I am, young man. Now, what's your name and what can I do for you? What toys can I bring for you this Christmas?"

"My name is Eric Marrin and I don't want any toys," he said soberly, staring at a coal-black button on the front of Santa's suit.

Santa gasped in surprise. "No toys? But every child wants toys for Christmas."

"Not me. I want something else. Something much more important."

Santa hooked his thumb under Eric's chin and tipped his head up. "And what is that?"

"I—I want a huge Christmas tree with twinkling lights. And I want our house all decorated with plastic reindeer on the roof and a big wreath on the door. I want Christmas cookies and hot cider. And Christmas carols on the stereo. And on Christmas Eve, I want to fall asleep in front of the fireplace and have my dad carry me up to bed. And on Christmas Day, I want a huge turkey dinner and cherry pie for dessert." The words had just tumbled out of his mouth and he'd been unable to stop them. Eric swallowed hard, knowing he was probably asking for the impossible. "I want it to be like when my mother lived with us. She always made Christmas special."

For a long moment, Santa didn't speak. Eric worried that he might toss him out of the Gingerbread Cottage for demanding too much. Toys were simple for a guy who owned his own toy factory, but Eric's request was so complicated. Still, if Raymond was right, this Santa was his best shot at granting his Christmas wish.

"My—my mom left us right before Christmas two years ago. And my dad doesn't know how to do Christmas right. Last year, we didn't even have a tree. And—and he wants to go skiing again, but if we're not home, we can't have a real Christmas! You can help me, can't you?"

"So you want your mother to come home for Christmas?"

"No," Eric said, shaking his head. "I know she can't come back. She's an actress and she travels a lot. She's in London now, doing a play. I see her in the summer for two weeks and she sends me postcards from all over. And—and I know you can't bring me a new mother because there's no way you can make a human in your toy factory. Not that I wouldn't like a new mother, but hey, I know she won't fit in the sleigh with all those toys and you'd never be able to get down the chimney carrying her

in your sack and what if my dad didn't like the kind you
brought and—''

"What exactly do you want?'' Santa asked, jumping in
the moment Eric took a breath.

"The best Christmas ever!'' he cried. "A Christmas
like it used to be when my mom was here.''

"That's a pretty big wish,'' Santa said.

Eric cast his gaze to the toes of his rubber boots. "I
know. But you're Santa. If you can't make it happen, who
can?''

He risked a glance up to find Santa smiling warmly.
"Do you have a letter for me, young man?''

Eric nodded. "I was going to put it in the mailbox.''

"Why don't you give it to me personally and I'll make
sure I read it right after Mrs. Claus and I finish our dinner.''

Reaching in his jacket pocket, Eric withdrew the pre-
cious letter. Did this mean that Santa would grant his
wish? Surely it must mean that he'd consider it. "Eric
Marrin,'' he murmured pointing to the return address, just
to make sure. "731 Hawthorne Road, Schuyler Falls, New
York. It's the last driveway before you get to the bridge.
The sign says Stony Creek Farm, Alex Marrin, owner.
That's my dad.''

"I'm sure it's on my map,'' Santa said. "I know I've
been to your house before, Eric Marrin.'' He patted Eric
on the back. "You're a good boy.''

Eric smiled. "I try,'' he said as he slid off Santa's lap.
"Oh, and if you hear I broke the rules coming to see you
tonight, maybe you could understand? I know I'm supposed to go home directly after school, but I really
couldn't ask my dad to bring me here. He's very busy
and I didn't want him to think that I—''

"I understand. Now, do you know how to get home?''

Eric nodded. The city bus would take him back in the direction of his school and he'd have to run the mile down Hawthorne Road to make it home before dinner. He'd already told Gramps he'd planned to play at Raymond's house after school and Raymond's mother would drive him home. He'd have to sneak into the house unnoticed, but his father usually worked in the stables until supper time. And Gramps was usually busy with dinner preparations, his attention fixed on his favorite cooking show while the pots bubbled over on the stove.

Eric waved goodbye to Santa and, to his delight, Santa tucked his letter safe inside his big red jacket. "Some of the kids at school say you aren't real, but I'll always believe in you."

With that, he hurried through the crowd and down the escalator to the first floor. When he'd finally reached the street, he took a deep breath of the crisp evening air. Fluffy snowflakes had begun to fall and the sidewalk was slippery. Eric picked up his pace, weaving in between holiday shoppers and after-work pedestrians.

The bus stop was on the other side of the town square. He paused only a moment to listen to the carolers and stare up at the huge Christmas tree, now dusted with snow. When he reached the bus stop, a long line had formed, but Eric was too excited to worry. So what if he got home a little late? So what if his father found out where he'd been? That didn't matter anymore.

All that mattered was that Eric Marrin was going to have the most perfect Christmas in the whole wide world. Santa was going to make it happen.

"I DON'T LIKE THIS. This whole thing smells like month-old halibut."

Holly Bennett glanced over at her assistant, Meghan

O'Malley, then sighed. "And last week you thought the doorman at our office building was working as an undercover DEA agent and our seventy-year-old janitor was an international terrorist. Meg, you have got to get over this obsession with the news. Reading ten newspapers a day is starting to make you paranoid!"

As she spoke, Holly's breath clouded in front of her face and a shiver skittered down her spine. She pulled her coat more tightly around her body, then let her gaze scan the picturesque town square. There was no denying that the situation was a little odd, but danger lurking in Schuyler Falls, New York? If she took a good look around, she would probably see the Waltons walking down the street.

"I like to be informed. Men find that sexy," Meghan countered, her Long Island accent thick and colorful, her bright red hair a beacon even in the evening light. "And you're entirely too trusting. You've lived in the big city for five years; it's time to wise up." She sighed and shook her head. "Maybe it's the mob. I knew it! We're going to be working for wise guys."

"We're two hundred miles north of New York City," Holly cried. "I don't think this is a hotbed of mob activity. Look around. We're in the middle of a Norman Rockwell painting." Holly turned slowly on the sidewalk to take in the gentle snowfall, the quaint streetlights, the huge Christmas tree sparkling with lights in the center of the square. She'd never seen anything quite so pretty. It was like a scene from *It's A Wonderful Life*.

One side of the square was dominated by a majestic old courthouse and the opposite by a department store right out of the 1920s called Dalton's, its elegant stone facade and wide plate-glass windows ablaze with holiday cheer. Small shops and restaurants made up the rest of the square, each and every one decked out for the Christmas season with fresh evergreen boughs and lush, red ribbon.

Meg surveyed the scene suspiciously, her eyes narrowing. "That's what they'd like us to think. They're luring us in, making us feel comfortable. It's like one of those stories where the town appears perfect on the surface but it's got a seamy underbelly that would—"

"Who is luring us in?" Holly demanded.

"Exactly my point," Meg said. "This morning, we get a mysterious letter with a huge check signed by some phantom client with very poor penmanship. We're given just a few hours to go home and pack, then take a train halfway across the state of New York and you don't even know who we're working for. Maybe it's the CIA. They celebrate Christmas, don't they?"

Holly glanced at Meg, then looked down at the letter clutched in her hand. The overnight missive had arrived in the Manhattan office of All The Trimmings just that morning at the very moment she'd learned her struggling business was about to finish yet another year in the red.

She'd started All The Trimmings five years ago and this Christmas had become a turning point. She was nearly twenty-seven years old and had all of $300 in her savings account. If her company didn't show at least a few dollars profit, Holly would be forced to close down the tiny office and try another line of work. Maybe go back to the profession she'd trained for and failed at first—interior design.

Though she had plenty of competitors, no one in the Christmas business worked harder than Holly Bennett. She was a Christmas consultant, holiday decorator, personal corporate Christmas shopper and anything else her clients required. When called upon, she'd even dressed a client's dog for a canine holiday party and baked doggy biscuits in the shape of candy canes.

She'd started off small, with residential installations, decorating New York town houses both inside and out. Her designs became known for unique themes and interesting materials. There'd been the butterfly tree she'd done for Mrs. Wellington, a huge Douglas fir covered with colorful paper butterflies. Or the decorations she'd done for Big Lou, King of the Used Cars, combining gold-sprayed auto parts ornaments and nuts and bolts garland. Over the next few years, she'd taken on corporate clients—a string of shopping malls on Long Island, a few boutiques in Manhattan—and the demand for her services had required a full-time assistant.

Holly had always loved Christmas. From the time she was a little girl, she'd anticipated the start of the season, officially beginning the moment Thanksgiving was over and ending on Christmas Day—her birthday. No sooner had her mother put away the Indian corn and Horn of Plenty centerpiece than she'd retrieve all the beautiful Christmas ornaments from the dusty old attic of their house in Syracuse. Next, Holly and her dad would cut down a tree and the whirl of decorating and shopping and cookie-baking wouldn't stop until midnight on the twenty-fifth, when she and her mother and father would tumble into their beds, exhausted but already planning for her next birthday and the Christmas that came with it.

It was the one time of year she felt special, like a princess, instead of the shy, unpopular girl she'd been. She'd done everything to make the holiday perfect, obsessed with the tiniest details, striving for perfection. Holly's mother had been the one to suggest that she turn her degree in interior design toward something more seasonal.

At first, Holly had been thrilled with the strange path

her career had taken and she'd doted over the designs for
her earlier clients. But lately, Christmas had become syn-
onymous with business and income, profits and pressure,
not happy memories of her childhood. After her parents
had moved to Florida, Holly usually spent the holidays
working, joining them once all her clients were in bed on
Christmas night.

Without a family Christmas, she'd gradually lost touch
with the spirit of the season. But it was impossible to
make the trip to Florida and still keep watch over her
business. So Christmas had turned into something she
barely tolerated and had grown to dread, filled with last-
minute details and loneliness. She sighed inwardly. What
she wouldn't give for a real family Christmas this year.

"I've got it!" Meg cried. "This guy we're working for
is in the witness protection program and he's left his family behind because he doesn't want to burden them
with—"

"Enough," Holly interrupted. "I'll admit, his request
for an immediate consultation is a bit unusual. But look
at the bright side, Meg. Now that all our other holiday
installations are complete, we really don't have that much
to do." She could certainly find time to make Christmas
perfect for a client who chose to pay her a $15,000 re-
tainer for a two-week project, even if he *was* in the witness protection program.

"Nothing to do?" Meg asked. "We've got six new
commercial installations with mechanized reindeers and
sleighs to maintain and you know how temperamental
those singing reindeer are. And that tree we did for Far-
ley's courtyard on Park Avenue is going to take a lot of
maintenance. If we get a stiff wind, all the decorations
will end up in the East River. Plus we've got a list of
corporate Christmas gifts we still need to shop for."

"We can't afford to turn this job down," Holly murmured. "I've already spent my inheritance keeping this business afloat and my parents aren't even dead yet!"

"So how are we supposed to know who we're meeting?" Meg asked.

"The check was from the TD One Foundation. And the letter says he'll be wearing a sprig of holly in his lapel."

That very moment, Holly saw a tall gentleman approaching with the requisite holly. She jabbed Meg in the side and they both smiled graciously. "No more cracks about the mob," she muttered.

"Miss Bennett? Miss O'Malley?"

"He knows our names!" Meg whispered. "He probably knows where we live. If we make a run for it now, we might be able to get to the train before he sets his goons on us."

He held out his hand and Holly took it, noticing the fine cashmere coat he wore and the expensive gloves. Her gaze rose to his face and she felt her breath drain from her body. If this man was a mobster, then he was the handsomest mobster she'd ever seen. His dark hair ruffled in the wind and his patrician profile looked like carved marble in the dim light from the street lamps.

"It's a pleasure to meet you," he said. "And thank you for coming on such short notice."

"Mr.—I'm sorry," Meg said, holding out her own hand. "I didn't catch your name."

His cool expression didn't change as he brushed off her indirect question. "My name isn't important or necessary."

"How did you know it was us?" Meg asked, her eyes narrowed in suspicion.

"I just have a few minutes to talk, so why don't we get down to business." He reached for a manila envelope tucked beneath his arm. "All the information is here," he said. "The contract is for $25,000. Fifteen for your time, ten for expenses. Personally, I think $25,000 is entirely too much, but then, it's not my decision. Of course, you'll be required to stay here in Schuyler Falls until the day after Christmas. That won't be a problem, will it?"

Startled by the odd demand, Holly wasn't sure how to respond. Whose decision was it and what decision was he talking about? "Usually we suggest a budget after we've done a design, and once that's approved, we work out a timetable for installation. I—I don't know what you want or where you want it and we're up against a tight deadline."

"Your brochure says 'We make Christmas perfect.' That's all he wants, a perfect Christmas."

"Who?" Holly asked.

"The boy. Ah, I believe his name is Eric Marrin. It's all in the file, Miss Bennett. Now, if you'll excuse me, I really must go. I have a car waiting for you just over there. If you have any problems with the contract, you can call the number listed on the front of the folder and I'll hire someone else to do the job. Miss Bennett, Miss O'Malley, have a merry Christmas."

With a curt nod, he turned on his heel and disappeared into the crowd of shoppers strolling through the square, leaving both Holly and Meg with their mouths agape. "Gorgeous," Meg murmured.

"He's a client," Holly said, still stinging from his abrupt manner. "And rude! Besides, you know I'm engaged."

Meg rolled her eyes. "You broke up with Stephan nearly a year ago and you haven't seen him since. He hasn't even called you. He's not much of a fiancé if you ask me."

''We didn't break up,'' Holly replied, starting off toward the car parked on the other side of the square. ''He told me to take all the time I needed to decide on his proposal. And he has contacted me. I had a message on my machine a few weeks ago. He said he'd call me after the holidays and that he had something very important to tell me.''

Meg grabbed her arm and pulled her to a stop. ''You don't love him, Holly. He's snooty and self-absorbed and he has absolutely no passion.''

''I *could* love him,'' Holly said, a defensive edge to her voice. ''And now that my business will be in the black, I'll have some independence. I won't be marrying him for his money, for a secure future. We'll be equals.''

Meg paused for a long moment, then groaned. ''Oh, I didn't want to tell you this,'' she muttered, ''especially right before the holidays. But I read something in the papers last month and—''

''If this is another story about underworld crime, I—''

''Stephan's engaged,'' Meg blurted out. ''That's probably what he wants to tell you. He's marrying the daughter of some really rich guy. They're getting married in June in the Hamptons.'' Meg slipped her arm around Holly's shoulders. ''I shouldn't have told you like this, but you have to put Stephan out of your life. It's over, Holly.''

''But—but *we* were engaged,'' Holly murmured, stunned at the news. ''I finally made my decision and—and—''

''And it wasn't right. Holly, why do you think it took you a whole year to decide? It's because you didn't love him. Someday you'll meet a man who'll sweep you off your feet, but that man wasn't supposed to be Stephan.'' She patted her back sympathetically. ''So, let's just focus on work, all right? We've got a new job that pays $15,000. Open that envelope and let's hear what we have to do.''

Numbly Holly tore open the envelope. In her heart, she knew Meghan was right. She didn't love Stephan, she never had. She'd only decided to accept his proposal because no one else had bothered asking. But the news still stung. Being rejected by a man—even a man you didn't love—was still humiliating.

She drew a shaky breath. So she'd pass this Christmas as a free woman—no family, no fiancé, nothing but work to occupy her time. Holly pulled out a sheaf of papers from the envelope. Clipped on top was a letter, written on wide-lined paper, in a childish scrawl with smeared lead pencil. She skimmed through it, then moaned softly, her troubles with Stephan suddenly pushed aside. ''Oh, my. Look at this.''

Meg snatched the letter from Holly's fingers and read it aloud. ''Dear Santa, my name is Eric Marrin and I am almost eight and I have only one Christmas wish.'' She glanced at Holly and grinned. ''W-U-S-H. I would like you to bring me a Christmas like me and my dad used— Y-O-U-S-T—to have when my mom lived at our house. She made Christmas...'' Meg frowned at the spelling. ''Seashell?''

Holly sighed. ''Special.'' She flipped through the rest of the papers, long lists of items suggested for Christmas gifts and decorations and special dinners and activities, all to be paid for by an unnamed benefactor.

Meg waved the letter under Holly's nose, her apprehension suddenly gone. ''You have to take this job, Holly. You can't let this little boy down. This is what Christmas is all about.'' She glanced around the square, then fixed her gaze on the department store. ''Dalton's,'' she murmured. "You know, I've read about Dalton's, last year in some upstate newspaper. The article said their Santa grants special wishes to children, but no one knows where the money comes from. Do you think that guy was—"

Holly shoved the papers back into the envelope. "I don't care where the money comes from. We have a job to do and I'm going to do it."

"What about our clients in the city?"

"You'll take the train back to the city tonight and take care of them, while I do the job here."

Meg smiled. "This will be good for you, Holly. No time to be lonely for your family, no time to think about that jerk, Stephan. An almost unlimited budget to make a perfect Christmas. It's like you've won the lottery or died and gone to Christmas heaven."

Maybe this was exactly what she needed to rediscover the spirit of the season! All the way up from the city, she'd stared out the train window and watched the picturesque Hudson Valley scenery pass by. And when they'd stepped off the train, she'd been transported to another world, where the commercialism of Christmas hadn't quite taken hold.

Here, people smiled as they passed on the street and children laughed. From every shop doorway, the sound of Christmas music drifted out on the chill night air, mixing with the jingle bells from a horse-drawn carriage that circled the square. "It is perfect," she murmured, the lyrics from "Silver Bells" drifting through her head. And spending Christmas in Schuyler Falls was a far sight better than passing the holiday buried in year-end tax reports for her accountant.

She drew a deep breath and smiled. "Maybe I'll have a merry Christmas after all."

THE ANCIENT ROLLS ROYCE turned off the main road into the winding driveway of Stony Creek Farm just as Holly finished rereading her contract. The ride from downtown Schuyler Falls was even more picturesque than the train ride upstate, if that was possible. The old downtown gave way to lovely neighborhoods with stately brick and clapboard homes, built as summer homes for wealthy New Yorkers in the early part of the century, those who enjoyed the waters of nearby Saratoga Springs. Then, the streetlights disappeared and the houses became fewer, set back from the winding road and nearly hidden by thickets of leafless trees.

Somewhere in the darkness, the Hudson River streamed by, the same river she saw from her high-rise apartment on the west side of Manhattan. But here it was different, more pristine, adding to the magical atmosphere. The chauffeur, George, kept up a steady stream of informative chatter, giving her the history of the town and its people, yet steadfastly refusing to reveal who had hired him. She did learn that Stony Creek Farm was one of the few active horse breeding farms left in the area, owned by the Marrin family, longtime residents of Schuyler Falls.

As they slowly approached the main house, Holly peered through the frosty car window. On either side of the driveway were long white barns flanked by well-maintained plank fences. The house wasn't nearly as grand as some she'd seen, but it was large and inviting with its white clapboard siding, deep porches and green shutters.

"Here you are, miss," George said as he pulled to a stop. "Stony Creek Farm. I'll wait out here to take you back to town if you'd like."

She nodded. They'd dropped Meg at the train station to catch the late train back and Holly had picked up her overnight bag from a locker there. But as the hour was late, she'd decided to find a hotel after she'd introduced herself to Eric Marrin.

In truth, now that she was here, Holly wasn't quite sure how to broach the subject of her assignment. Her contract expressly forbid any mention of who'd hired her or who was paying the bill, not that she knew herself. But for all the Marrins knew, she was a complete stranger intruding on their lives. "Why don't you wait at the end of the driveway," she said. With no visible transportation back to town, Eric Marrin and his father would be compelled to invite her inside.

George hopped out of the car and ran around to open her door. As she stepped out, she didn't see any sign of Christmas, no wreath on the door, no lighted tree shining through a front window. Holly slowly climbed the front steps, then reached out for the brass door knocker. She snatched her hand back. What was she supposed to say?

"Hi, I'm here to grant your Christmas wish." She swallowed hard. "My name is Holly Bennett and I've been sent by Santa Claus." She was allowed to say she worked for the fat guy in the red suit, that much her contract did state.

"This is crazy," she muttered, turning around. A cold wind whipped around her feet and she tugged the lapels of her coat up around her face. "They're not going to let a perfect stranger in the house."

But the prospect of finally turning a profit was too much to resist. Perhaps she could even give Meg a well-deserved bonus this year. Gathering her resolve, Holly reached out and pushed the doorbell instead. A dog barked inside, and a few seconds later, the door swung open. The light from the foyer framed a small figure, a pale-haired boy with wide brown eyes and a curious expression. His large black dog stood next to him, eyeing Holly suspiciously. This had to be Eric Marrin.

"Hi," he said, his hand resting on the dog's head.

"Hi," Holly replied nervously.

"My dad's still in the barn. He'll be in soon."

"I'm not here to see your dad. Are you Eric?"

The boy nodded.

Holly held out her hand and smiled. "I—I'm…I'm your Christmas angel. Santa sent me to make all your Christmas dreams come true." She was sure the words would sound ridiculous once they left her mouth, but from the look on Eric's face, she couldn't fault her choice. An expression of pure joy suffused his features and the dog wagged his tail and barked.

"Wait here," he cried. The boy raced off into the house and returned a few moments later. He shrugged into his jacket, tugged on his mittens and grabbed her hand. "I knew you'd come," he said, his voice breathless with excitement.

"Where are we going?" she asked as he dragged her down the front steps, the dog trailing after them.

"To see my dad. You have to tell him we can't go to Colorado for Christmas. He'll listen to you. You're an angel."

They followed a snow-covered path toward the nearest barn, the cold and damp seeping through Holly's designer pumps. A real angel wouldn't mind the wet shoes, but they were her favorite pair and she'd spent a week's salary on them. She made a note to herself to use part of her budget for some cold weather essentials, like waterproof boots and socks, a necessity while working for a client who didn't bother shoveling the snow.

"Did you talk to Santa?" Eric asked. "He must have

read my letter right away. I only gave it to him a few days ago.''

Holly hesitated for a moment, then decided to maintain the illusion. "Yes, I did speak to Santa. And he told me personally to give you a perfect Christmas."

When they reached the barn, Eric grabbed the latch on the double door, heaved the doors open and showed her inside. A wide aisle ran the length of the barn, covered in a thin layer of straw and lit from above. "Dad!" Eric yelled. "Dad, she's here. My Christmas angel is here."

He hurried along the stalls, peering inside, and Holly followed him, steeling herself for his father's reaction. What she wasn't prepared for was her own reaction. A tall, slender man suddenly stepped out of a stall in front of her and she jumped back, pressing her palm to her chest to stop a scream. She'd expected someone older, maybe even middle-aged. But this man wasn't even thirty!

Holly looked up into the bluest eyes she'd ever seen in her life, bright and intense, the kind of blue that could make a girl melt, or cut her to the quick. He was tall, well over six feet, his shoulders broad and his arms finely muscled from physical labor. He wore scuffed work boots, jeans that hugged his long legs and a faded corduroy shirt with the sleeves turned up. Her eyes fixed on a piece of straw, caught in his sun-streaked hair.

He took a long look at her, then glanced over his shoulder at his son who continued to search each stall. "Eric?"

The little boy turned and ran back to them both. "She's here, Dad. Santa sent me an angel." He pointed to his father. "Angel, this is my dad, Alex Marrin. Dad, this is my Christmas angel."

She fought the urge to reach out and rake her hands through his hair, brushing away the straw and restoring perfection to an already perfect picture of masculine beauty. Holly coughed softly, realizing that she'd forgotten to breathe. She struggled to speak beneath his piercing gaze. "I—I've been sent by Santa," she said in an overly bright tone. "I'm here to make all your dreams come true." She sucked in a sharp breath. "I—I mean, all *Eric's* dreams. All Eric's *Christmas* dreams."

She watched as his gaze raked along her body, boldly, suspiciously. A shiver skittered down her spine and she wanted to turn and run. For all Eric's excitement at her arrival, she saw nothing but mistrust in this man's expression. But she held her ground, unwilling to let him intimidate her.

Suddenly Alex Marrin's expression softened and he laughed out loud, a sound she found unexpectedly alluring. "This is some kind of joke, right? What are you going to do? Start up the music and peel off your clothes?" He reached out and flicked his finger at the front of her coat. "What do you have on under there?"

Holly gasped. "I beg your pardon!"

"Who sent you? The boys down at the feed store?" He turned and glanced over his shoulder. "Pa, get out here! Did you order me an angel?"

A man's head popped out of a nearby stall, his weathered face covered with a rough gray beard. He moved to stand in the middle of the aisle, leaning on a pitchfork and shaking his head.

"She's my angel," Eric insisted. "Not some lady from the feed store."

The old man chuckled to himself. "Naw, I didn't send you anything. But if I were you, I wouldn't be refusing that delivery." He winked at Eric. "We could use an angel 'round this place."

"That's my gramps," Eric explained.

"Who sent you?" Alex Marrin demanded.

"Santa sent her," Eric replied. "I went to see him down at Dalton's and I—"

Alex's attention jumped to his son. "You went to see Santa? When was this?"

Eric kicked at a clump of straw, his expression glum. "The other day. After school. I just had to go, Dad. I had to give him my letter." He took Holly's hand. "She's here to give us a Christmas like we used to have. You know, when Mom was…"

Alex Marrin's jaw tightened and his expression grew hard. "Go back to the house, Eric. And take Thurston with you. I'll be in to talk to you in a few minutes."

"Don't send her away, Dad," Eric pleaded. His father gave him a warning glare and the little boy ran out of the barn, the exchange observed by his glowering grandfather. The old man cursed softly and stepped back into the stall. When the door slammed behind Eric, Alex Marrin turned his attention back to Holly.

"All right," he said. "Who are you? And who sent you?"

"My name is Holly Bennett," she replied, reaching into her purse for a business card. "See? All The Trimmings. We do professional decorating and event planning for the Christmas holidays. I was hired to give your son his Christmas wish. I'm to work for you through Christmas day."

"Hired by whom?"

"I—I'm afraid I can't say. My contract forbids it."

"What is this? Charity? Or maybe some busybody's idea of generosity?"

"No!" Holly said. "Not at all." She reached in her coat pocket and took out Eric's letter, then carefully unfolded it. "Maybe you should read this."

Marrin quickly scanned the letter, then raked his hands

through his hair and leaned back against a stall door. All his anger seemed to dissolve, his energy sapped and his shoulders slumped. "You must think I'm a terrible father," he said, his voice cold.

"I—I don't know you," Holly replied, reaching out to touch his arm. The instant she grazed his skin, a frisson of electricity shot through her fingers. She snatched them away and shoved her hand into her pocket. "I've already been paid. If you send me away without completing my duties, I'll have to return the money."

He cursed softly, then grabbed her hand and pulled her along toward the door. Holly wasn't sure whether to resist or go along with him. Was he going to toss her out on her ear? Or did she still have time to argue her case?

"Pa, I'll be back in a few minutes," he muttered. "I've got some business to take care of with this angel."

2

_____

"I WANT HER TO STAY!"

Alex ground his teeth as he stared at his son standing on the other side of his bed. Eric, dressed in his cowboy pajamas, had folded his arms over his chest, set his chin intractably and refused to meet Alex's eyes. He used to see Renee in his son, in the dark eyes and wide smile. But more and more, he was starting to see himself, especially in Eric's stubborn nature. "I know I've made some mistakes since your mother left and, I promise, I'll try to make things better. We don't need this lady to give us a nice Christmas."

"She's not a lady," Eric said with a pout. "She's an angel. _My_ angel."

Alex sat down on the edge of the bed and drew back the covers. "Her name is Holly Bennett. She gave me her business card. When was the last time you heard of an angel who had a business card?"

"It could happen," Eric said defensively. "Besides, her name doesn't make a difference. It's what she can do that counts."

"What can she do that I can't?" Alex asked. "I can put up a Christmas tree and tack up some garland." He patted the mattress and Eric reluctantly crawled beneath the covers.

"But you can't bake cookies and make ornaments and—and—the last time Gramps made turkey it tasted like old shoes!'' He slouched down and pulled the covers up to his chin. "If you haven't noticed, Dad, she's really, *really* pretty. Like supermodel pretty. And she smells good, too. She's mine and I want to keep her!''

Alex didn't need to be reminded of the obvious. If she hadn't introduced herself as a mortal being, he might have believed Holly Bennett truly was heaven sent. She had the face of an angel, a wide, sensual mouth and bright green eyes ringed with thick lashes. Her wavy blond hair had shimmered in the soft light of the barn, creating a luminous halo around her head and accentuating her high cheekbones and perfectly straight nose.

No, that fact didn't get past him. Nor did his reaction to her beauty—sudden and stirring, almost overwhelming his senses. Over the past two years he'd managed to ignore almost every woman he'd come in contact with, not that there had been many. Running a horse breeding operation didn't put him in the path of the opposite sex very often.

He'd ignored social invitations and community events, secluding himself on the farm day and night and losing himself in his work. The last woman he'd touched was Eric's teacher, Miss Green, and that was a benign handshake at the parent-teacher conferences. Never mind that Miss Green was fifty-seven years old and smelled of chalk dust and rose water.

But Holly Bennett wasn't a spinster schoolteacher and she was hard to ignore. His fingers tingled as he remembered touching her, wrapping her delicate hand in his as he dragged her out of the barn. She was waiting downstairs at this very moment, waiting for him to decide her fate, and his mind was already starting to conjure excuses to touch her again.

"She could stay in the guest room," Eric suggested.

Alex leveled a perturbed look at his son. "I'm not allowing a perfect stranger to—"

"Angel," Eric corrected.

"All right, a perfect angel, to stay in our house."

"Then she can stay in the tack house. No one's stayed there since Gramps moved back into the house. *He* thinks she's pretty and nice."

"How do you know?" Alex said, raising an eyebrow.

"I can just tell." His son set his mouth in a stubborn straight line.

Alex covered his eyes with his hands and moaned. If he sent Holly Bennett packing, Eric would never forgive him. And he wouldn't hear the end of it from his father. Aw, hell, maybe it wasn't such a bad idea having her around. He hated stringing lights on the tree. The smell of evergreen made him sneeze. And he was more comfortable with curry combs than cookie cutters.

Besides, Christmas had always reminded him of Renee. Every ornament, every decoration brought back memories of their time together, time when they'd been a happy family with a bright future. The week after she'd left, he'd thrown out every reminder of Christmas she'd brought into the house, vowing to discard anything that brought thoughts of her betrayal.

But here was a chance to begin anew, to create Christmas traditions only he and Eric shared. Sure, Holly the Angel would be around, but she was nothing more than an employee, a helping hand during a busy season. And he was curious to learn who was paying her salary, a secret he might learn given time. "All right," Alex said. "She has three days to prove herself and if everything's going all right, she can stay."

"Then we're not going skiing in Colorado?"

He sent his son a grudging smile. "No, we're not going

to Colorado. But you're going to have to deal with her. I'm not going take care of her the same way I have to take care of Thurston and the horses. She's your angel.''

Eric hit him full force against the chest, throwing himself at Alex and wrapping his arms around his father's neck. The boy gave him an excruciating hug and beamed up at him. ''Thanks, Dad. Can I go tell her?''

Alex ruffled Eric's pale hair, a flood of parental love warming his blood, then kissed his son on the cheek. It took so little to make Eric happy. How could he think of refusing him even a bit of joy? ''Crawl back under the covers and I'll tuck you in. Then I'll go down and tell your angel.''

Eric gave him another quick hug, then scrambled back between the sheets. As he did every night, Alex tucked the blankets around his son, then tickled his stomach. ''Who loves you the most?''

''You do!'' Eric cried.

Alex brushed the hair out of Eric's eyes, then stood. But as he walked to the door, his son's voice stopped him. ''Dad? Do you ever miss Mom?''

His hand froze on the doorknob and Alex turned around. He wasn't sure what to say. Did he miss the fighting, the constant anger that bubbled between them? Did he miss the sick feeling he got every time she went into the city, knowing she was meeting another man? No, he didn't. But he did miss the contentment he saw in his son's eyes whenever Renee was near. ''Your mom is very talented. She had to leave so that she could be the very best actress she could. But that doesn't mean that she doesn't love you just as much as I do.''

Though his question hadn't been answered, Eric smiled, then sank back against the pillows. ''Night, Dad.''

Alex released a tightly held breath as he slowly de-

scended the stairs, wondering at how he'd managed to
dodge yet another bullet. Sooner or later, Eric would demand explanations and Alex wasn't sure what to tell him.
So far, he'd always managed to evade the truth. But could
he tell an outright lie to his son?

He turned into the library and stopped short. Holly sat
primly on a leather wing chair staring at the dying embers
of a fire in the fireplace across the room. She was like a
vision from paradise and Alex found himself tongue-tied.
She'd removed her coat and tossed it over the back of the
chair, revealing a pretty red jacket, cinched in at her tiny
waist and a slim black skirt that revealed impossibly long
legs. He'd never met a woman quite as cool and sophisticated as her. But though she appeared to be all business,
there was an underlying allure that was hard to ignore.
"I'm sorry to keep you waiting," he muttered. "If you'll
just tell me where your things are, I'll get you settled."

She straightened at the sound of his voice then neatly
crossed her legs. Alex stood beside his desk and let his
gaze drift along the sweet curve of her calf. When she
cleared her throat, he snapped back to reality and silently
scolded himself. If Holly Bennett would be hanging
around this holiday season, he'd have to prevent all future
fantasizing!

"Thank you," she said in a quiet voice, "for allowing
me to stay."

"I suppose I should be thanking you," Alex replied.
"Eric requested you be offered a guest room, but—"

"Oh, no!" Holly cried. "I have a budget. I can afford
to stay at a hotel. And I'll rent a car to get back and
forth."

"If you'll let me finish," Alex said. "I agreed that you
can stay for the next three days. I can't imagine you'll
need any more time than that. And you can stay in the

tack house. It's quite nice. There're a couple of guest rooms with private baths and small kitchenettes. And you can use the pickup to get around. I can use my dad's old truck.''

"But I've been hired to stay through Christmas day,'' she replied. She stared down at her lap, then glanced back up at him. "I know this is a little strange, me barging into your lives. Believe me, this is not the typical job for me. But I do intend to do it right and that will take more than three days.''

"How long can it take to put up a Christmas tree and a few strings of lights?'' he demanded.

She looked at him disdainfully, as if he'd just asked her to build the Queen Mary III overnight. "Actually, Mr. Marrin, the job will take quite a bit of time and attention. You have no decorations up and, from what your father tells me, you don't have any in storage. Between the exteriors and the interiors, there are at least three days of *planning* to be done. And with the budget, I can do some very special things. And I've got baking to do and menus to plan and if you'd like to throw a party or two I'm perfectly capable of—''

He held out his hand to stop her. "Slow down, Betty Crocker.''

"Martha Stewart,'' she muttered.

"What?''

"Betty Crocker is a face on a cake box. I'm really much more like Martha Stewart.'' She sighed impatiently and stared at her hands.

"All right. Why don't we just see if everything goes all right, then we'll talk about extending your…earthly incarnation. But first, maybe you'd like to tell me who's financing your visit.''

She shrugged her delicate shoulders. ''I told you, I don't know.''

''Don't know, or can't say?''

''Both,'' Holly murmured.

A long silence spun out between them as Alex watched her intently. She shifted in her chair, and for a moment, he thought she might bolt. ''She left two years ago,'' he said, meeting her shocked gaze coolly. ''Four days before Christmas. That's what you've wanted to ask, isn't it?''

''It—it's none of my business,'' Holly replied as if questioning her curiosity was nothing more than an insult. ''I don't think it's necessary for me to become personally involved in your lives to do my job. I'm here to give your son, and you, a perfect Christmas. I'm very good at my job, Mr. Marrin, and I don't think you'll be disappointed.''

''This is for my son,'' Alex replied. ''Not me. Eric misses his mother around the holidays. Things have been difficult for him. He doesn't see much of her.''

The meaning of his words couldn't have been clearer. He wasn't looking for another wife and he didn't want Holly Bennett to pretend to be Eric's mother. He watched as she rose to her feet, her demeanor growing more distant with each passing moment. ''If that's all, then I'll be saying good night. I've got a busy day in front of me tomorrow. If you'll just point me in the direction of the tract house—''

Alex chuckled. ''*Tack* house. It's where we keep the saddles and bridles. We call that tack.''

''I'm going to be sleeping in a storage shed?'' she asked.

''I assure you, Miss Bennett, it's quite nice. Now, where are your things?'' Alex asked.

''My things?''

"Your halo and harp? You know, all your angel accoutrements?"

"My luggage is in the car. The driver is parked at the end of the driveway."

Alex nodded. "I'll go get your bags and then I'll show you to your room."

"Mr. Marrin, I—"

"Alex," he said, pulling the library door open for her. He placed his hand on her back as she passed, then helped her into her coat. His palms lingered on her shoulders for a few seconds, her silken hair brushing his skin. Reason told him he'd have to draw his hands away, but it had been so long since he'd touched a woman, smelled the fresh scent of a woman's hair, fought the overwhelming longing to make love to—

Alex opened the front door and showed her out, drawing a deep breath of the crisp night air. The cold revived him, clearing his mind. Granted, she was beautiful—and thoughtful—and unquestionably single-minded. But the last thing he needed in his life was a woman and all the trouble that came along with a romantic relationship.

No, he'd keep his distance from this angel. And if he knew what was good for him, he'd put any devilish fantasies right out of his head.

"SHE'S AN ANGEL. I SWEAR!"

For a moment, Holly wasn't sure where she was. Were the voices part of a dream? Slowly everything came back to her. She'd spent the night in Alex Marrin's tack house. Though she'd anticipated a storage shed, her room looked more like a quaint B & B than a barn. A beautiful field-stone fireplace dominated one wall of her bedroom, while the others were paneled with warm knotty pine. Across from the iron bed was a tiny galley kitchen and a white-washed table and just outside the door was a pretty sitting area, decorated with old harnesses and riding prints and yellowed photos of very large horses.

"She doesn't have wings," said an unfamiliar voice.

Holly slowly opened her eyes. When her vision focused, she found two little faces staring at her from close range. One she recognized as Eric Marrin. The other, a gap-toothed, freckle-faced boy, observed her as if she were an interesting lab specimen, pickled in formaldehyde and floating in a jar.

"Can she fly?" he said, lisping slightly through his missing front teeth.

"Jeez, Kenny, she's not that kind of angel!" Eric said. "She's a Christmas angel. They're different."

"What's wrong with her hair?" Kenny asked.

Holding back a smile, Holly sleepily pushed up on one elbow. She looked at Eric then Kenny. "Good morning." Kenny jumped back from the bed, a blush staining his cheeks, but Eric happily plopped down on the patchwork coverlet.

"This is my friend, Kenny. He lives down the road. We go to school together."

Holly ran her fingers through her tangled hair and yawned. Judging by the feeble light coming through the window, it was still well before eight. The boys were dressed in jackets, both carrying backpacks. She groaned softly. Though her bed had been wonderfully cozy, her night had been plagued with strange and disjointed dreams. Unbidden images of Alex Marrin had been punctuated with a recurring nightmare that had her endlessly untangling tinsel and searching for the single bad bulb in a mile-long string of lights.

Why did Alex Marrin fascinate her so? Until yesterday evening, she'd been ready to spend her life with Stephan!

Yes, Alex was incredibly handsome. Perhaps it was the rugged, salt-of-the-earth image. Or maybe it was the wounded look she saw, deep in his eyes, the wariness that seemed to pervade his lean body whenever he looked at her. He seemed to exude excitement and a little bit of danger.

"Does she have a magic wand?" Kenny asked, regarding her from beneath a scruffy wool cap.

Eric rolled his eyes. "Angels don't have magic wands. Fairy godmothers do. And wizards."

Holly should have explained to the boys that "Christmas angel" had been a metaphorical reference, a way to explain her place in this whole scheme as granter of wishes. She could have just as easily called herself a Christmas genie. "Why don't you just call me Holly," she suggested, too sleepy to make sense of her new job.

"We brought you breakfast, Holly," Eric said, retrieving a battered cookie sheet from a nearby table and setting it on the bed. "Dad says I'm in charge of feeding you. Cap'n Crunch, Tang and toast with grape jelly. After you're finished we'll show you around the farm. I've got my own pony and a pinball machine in my bedroom."

"Here you are!"

Holly glanced up to find Alex Marrin looming in the doorway of her room. He was dressed much as he had been the previous night, in rugged work clothes and a faded canvas jacket. But his hair was still damp from a shower and he was freshly shaven. She scrambled to pull the covers up over the gaping neck of her camisole, then felt a flush of embarrassment warm her cheeks.

"You're late for school," Alex said to the boys. "Come on, I'll drive you."

"But Holly needs a tour," Eric said. "We always give company a tour."

A crooked smile touched Alex's lips and he glanced at Holly. "She's still half asleep." Eric gave his father a pleading look. "I'll show her around," he finally replied, "when I get back. Now let's move!"

The boys called out a quick goodbye, then rushed out. Alex's gaze met hers for a long moment and she tried to read the thoughts behind the enigmatic blue eyes. "I'll just be a few minutes. Enjoy your breakfast." With that, he turned and followed the kids. With a soft moan, Holly stumbled out of bed, wrapped the quilt around her shoulders and crossed to the window, watching as they walked past the house to the driveway beyond.

Of course she was fascinated with him. He was the first man to wander into the general vicinity of her boudoir in nearly a year! And though Stephan had always taken his manly duties quite seriously, he'd never set her pulse racing the way Alex Marrin did. Perhaps it had been fate that had kept her from accepting Stephan's proposal. Perhaps, deep down inside, she knew there was a man out there who could make her feel…Holly groped for the right word. Passion?

She leaned against the windowsill and pressed her nose to the cold glass. She had never considered herself a passionate woman, the kind of woman who could toss aside all her inhibitions and give herself over to a man's touch. But then, maybe she hadn't been touched in just the right way.

"And you think Alex Marrin is the man to do it?" Holly shook her head, then wandered back to the bed. Sure, there was a certain irresistible charm about him. The easy masculine grace of his walk, the casual way he wore his clothes and combed his hair with his fingers. Any woman would find that attractive.

But there was more, Holly mused. When she looked at

Alex Marrin, unbidden and unfamiliar desire surged up inside of her, disturbing thoughts of soft moans and tangled limbs and overwhelming need. Her stomach fluttered, but Holly knew the sensation would never be satisfied with Tang and Cap'n Crunch.

"He's a client," she murmured to herself. Though that wasn't entirely true, since the mysterious benefactor was the one paying her salary. Still, she'd be better off if she kept her distance. This was strictly professional! With a soft oath, she crossed back to the bed, picked up her cereal bowl and took a big bite.

"Ugggghhh!" The sweetness of the cereal made her gag and she spit it out, wiped her tongue with the paper napkin, then guzzled down the tart and barely dissolved Tang. The toast was just as bad, cold and overloaded with jelly. Holly dropped it back on the plate and wiped her hands. "At least I won't have to worry about those fifteen holiday pounds."

By the time a soft knock sounded on her door, nearly twenty minutes had passed. She'd dressed, restored some order to her hair and applied a quick bit of mascara and lipstick. Holly took one last look in the mirror then called out. Slowly Alex opened the door, but he ventured only a few steps inside. "You're not ready," he said, taking in her choice of wardrobe, the cashmere sweater set, the wool skirt and her water-stained leather pumps.

Holly glanced down at her clothes, then back up. "I'm sorry. This is all I brought. I thought I'd go out today and get some more casual clothes."

"Those shoes won't do." Alex stalked out of the room and returned a few moments later with a pair of tall rubber boots. He dropped them at her feet. "Put those on."

Holly glanced down at the high rubber boots, encrusted with who knows what and at least six or seven sizes too big. There were probably spiders lurking inside their dark depths. She crinkled her nose and shook her head. "Thank you, but I think I'd be more comfortable in my own shoes."

He shrugged. "Suit yourself. We'll start with the barns." Alex stepped aside and motioned her out the door.

"Actually, I don't need to see the barns," Holly said, grabbing her coat, "unless you'd like them to be decorated, too. I really need to start in the house. I've got to measure the rooms and decide on an approach. I think we should stay with more primitive, country themes. Besides, I'm really not very good with animals—dogs, cats, goats, horses."

He gave her a puzzled look. "I think the standard decorations would be fine," he said, striding out of the tack house. "You know, shiny balls and tinsel garland."

She closed the door behind her and shrugged into her coat. "No! I meant real animals. They don't like me. As a child I had a rather unfortunate encounter with a Guernsey cow."

"This is a horse farm," he said. "If you plan on staying until Christmas, it'll be hard to avoid the animals."

Resigned to her fate, Holly hurried after him, her heels sinking into the soggy snow along the path. They began with a tour of the barns, Alex showing her the indoor arena first. She stood on the bottom rung of the gate and watched as Alex's father ran a horse in circles around the perimeter of the arena.

"Why does he have the horse on a leash?"

Again, she caught him smiling. "That's called a lunge line," he said. "It gives him more control. Some of our horses don't need it."

Their tour didn't stop for long. He turned away from the arena and led her back to the main aisle of the barn.

"How many horses do you have?" she asked.

"We have about seventy horses on the farm," Alex replied. "Just over forty thoroughbred broodmares, twenty-seven yearlings that we'll sell at auction in January, a few retired stallions, a few draft horses and some saddlebreds. In the summer we can have another twenty horses that board and train here while they're racing at Saratoga. They use the outer barns and the track."

"That seems like a lot of horses." Holly sighed. "Actually, one horse is one too many for me. I once had this horrible experience with a horse, the kind that pulls the carriages around Central Park. It was frightening."

He forced a smile. "We're really a small operation compared to some. In my grandfather's day, we were a lot bigger. But we've got a good reputation and great bloodlines. Our yearlings fetch a high price at auction."

He reached in his shirt pocket and handed Holly a few sugar cubes, then pointed to the horse in the next stall. "That's Scirocco, grandson of Secretariat. He's one of the old men we keep here and he's retired from fatherhood. He's got a sweet tooth and he likes the ladies."

"If you don't use him how do you get…horsey babies?"

"Foals. And that's all done scientifically now," Alex said. "These days, you don't need the actual stallion, just what he has to offer."

Holly frowned. "You mean he doesn't get to—"

Alex shook his head. "Nope."

With a frown, Holly held the sugar between her fingers, just out of the horse's reach. "That seems so cruel. What about his needs?" Though she'd never liked animals and considered them smelly and unpredictable and frightening, she couldn't help but feel sorry for the old horse— even though he did have very big teeth.

"Believe me," he muttered. "A male doesn't always have to follow his…instincts." Though the discussion was clearly about a horse, Holly couldn't help but wonder if there might be another meaning to Alex's words.

Alex put the cube in her palm and pushed her hand nearer. The moment the horse nibbled the sugar, she snatched her fingers away. "Animals hate me," she said nervously, her attention diverted by the gentle touch of his hand. "Dogs bark at me and cats shed. I—I won't even tell you about my run-ins with chickens and ducks."

"Funny, he seems to be quite taken with you," Alex replied, capturing her gaze with his. For what seemed like an eternity, neither one of them moved. Holly wasn't even sure her heart was still beating.

Somehow, she didn't think Alex was talking about the horse this time, either. Uneasy with the silence, she braced her hand on the edge of the stall door and tried to appear casual and composed, as if handsome men stared at her every day of the week and she barely noticed. "If we're through here, I think we should—ouch!"

Holly jumped back, a sharp pain shooting through her finger. But she moved so quickly that she didn't notice the danger lurking right behind her. Her foot sank into a warm pile of horse manure. She tried to gracefully extract herself but when her heel struck the smooth floor beneath, her foot skidded out from under her. With a soft cry, she landed on her backside, right in the middle of the pile of poop.

The smell that wafted up around her made her eyes water and Holly moaned softly, not sure how to cover her embarrassment. She glanced down at her finger and found it bleeding. "He bit me!" she cried, holding out her hand.

She heard a low whinny come from the stall and saw the vicious horse watching her with a mocking eye and a smug smile, his lip curling over his huge fangs. Alex held out his hand and helped her struggle to her feet. "I'm sorry," he muttered through clenched teeth. "Scirocco can be a little aggressive when it comes to treats. And that should have been cleaned up."

Holly winced as she tried to shake the filthy shoe off her foot. But the horse poop had seeped inside and it stubbornly clung to her toes. "Just because you haven't had sex for a few years, doesn't mean you have to take it out on me!" She glanced up to find Alex looking at her with an astonished expression. Holly felt her face flame. "I—I meant the horse, not you."

"I'm sure you did." With an impatient curse, Alex scooped her up in his arms and carried her across the barn to a low bench.

She might have protested, if she hadn't enjoyed the feeling of his arms cradling her body. He lifted her as if she weighed nothing more than a feather. But before she could start to like the feeling too much, Alex dropped her to her feet, causing her knees to buckle slightly.

"Sit," he ordered.

Holly twisted to see the damage done to her favorite coat, hoping to hide the flush that had warmed her cheeks. But standing on one foot, she almost lost her balance again. Alex grabbed the collar of her coat to steady her, then slipped it off her shoulders and tossed it over a nearby stall door. He shrugged out of his own jacket and held it out to her.

When Holly pushed her arms into the sleeves she could still feel the heat from his body in the folds of fabric. His scent drifted up around her, a mix of soap and fresh air and horses, a welcome relief from her previous *parfum* and a reminder of the time spent in his arms. "Thank you," she murmured.

"Now, sit," Alex said. He knelt down in front of her and gently removed her ruined shoe. The mess had seeped through her panty hose and stuck in between her toes. He circled her calf with his hands, then slowly ran his palms toward her ankle. But the imagined caress ended abruptly when he tore through the nylon at her calf. She sucked in a sharp breath as he skimmed her stocking down along her leg and bared her foot. "You should have worn those boots."

"I told you animals hate me," she reminded him, a bit breathlessly.

"I'm sure Scirocco had this all planned. He's grown to be quite a curmudgeon in his retirement and, in truth, has a real talent for torturing our female guests." With that, he pushed to his feet and disappeared into a small alcove nearby. She heard water running, then leaned back against the barn wall.

"They say horse poop is the best beauty treatment for the skin."

She glanced to her right and saw Alex's father peeking out from a nearby stall. Though he'd introduced himself the previous night, they hadn't shared but a few words. But Holly already knew she'd found a friend in Jed Marrin. The man had a devilish sense of humor and an easygoing manner that his son seemed to lack.

"You know, Miss Bennett, you're the first woman we've had at this farm in two years. And I don't mind saying, you're a far sight nicer to look at than these old nags."

"Thank you, Mr. Marrin."

He winked. "You can call me Jed if I can call you Holly."

"All right, Jed."

He nodded to her foot. "Around here we call that a Stony Creek pedicure."

A small giggle slipped from her throat and Holly stretched her leg out in front of her, turning it from side to side. "Once I tell all my friends in the city, I'm sure you'll be able to package some of this stuff and make a million."

"Well, we got plenty of inventory," he said. "And I account for all of it, it seems."

Alex returned with a bucket of soapy water, a first-aid kit, and the pair of boots she'd refused just minutes before. "Except for that little item you missed in front of Scirocco's stall," he said. He gave his father an irritated look and the old man winked at Holly again, then went back to his work in the stall. Holly watched him until she felt Alex's hands cup her foot. Slowly he placed it in the bucket of warm water and began to rub.

Holly gulped nervously, wonderful sensations surging up her leg. She'd never considered the foot an erogenous zone, but with her pounding heart and her swimming head, Holly knew she'd be forced to revise her opinion. What Alex Marrin was doing to her toes was simply sinful! Biting back a moan of pleasure, she scrambled for a topic of conversation.

"How long have you lived here—on the farm?" she murmured, her voice cracking slightly.

"My whole life," Alex said, moving his hands up to her ankle. "My great-grandfather owned this place before he turned it over to my grandfather, who turned it over to my father, who turned it over to me. It's been in the family since the early 1900s. There used to be lots of breeders and boarders in the area, but now, we're one of the last. Most of the thoroughbreds are raised south of the Mason-Dixon line."

He took her foot from the bucket and dried it with a rough towel, then slipped her foot into the rubber boot. She kicked off her other shoe and the second boot followed the first.

"Now that we've tended to your bruised pride, let's see about that finger." Alex took her left hand and gently examined her finger. He pulled a bandanna from his jeans and wrapped her wound. "It's not so bad. I've got antiseptic and bandages here."

"Shouldn't I get a shot?" she asked.

He sent a withering glare Scirocco's way. "Don't worry, he's not rabid."

He bent over her finger, his clumsy attempts to render first aid undeniably charming. Holly smiled inwardly. It felt good to have a man worry over her, even a man as indifferent and aloof as Alex Marrin. Maybe getting bitten by a horse and sitting in horse manure wasn't such a bad trade-off for his attentions.

He carefully washed her finger with a soapy rag, then doused it with antiseptic. A bandage followed. "There," he said. "All better." Alex pressed his lips to her fingertip.

Holly blinked in surprise and when he glanced up, she could see he was similarly startled by his own action.

"I—I'm sorry," Alex stammered, suddenly flustered. "I'm so used to fixing Eric's cuts and scrapes, it's force of habit."

She smiled and withdrew her hand. "It does feel better." Holly drew a shaky breath.

He nodded, his jaw suddenly tight, his eyes distant. Alex cleared his throat, clearly uneasy in her presence. "Well, I should really get back to work," he murmured. "The house is empty. You can look around, get your bearings. Make yourself a decent breakfast."

With that, he turned and walked out, leaving Holly still wrapped in his coat, her finger still throbbing and her leg still tingling from his touch. She clomped toward the door in the oversized boots, wondering if there'd ever come a time when she'd understand Alex Marrin. In the end, she decided it didn't matter. She was here to do a job and nothing Alex did or said—including kissing her fingers or massaging her feet—would change her life in the least.

3

"SHE'S A PRETTY LITTLE thing. And don't tell me you haven't noticed. Every time I turn around, you're touchin' her or starin' at her. Last night at supper you almost tripped all over yourself helping to clear the table. You never do that when I cook."

"Maybe if you cooked as good as she does, I would," Alex murmured, not loud enough to reach his father two stalls away. He turned his focus back to the dandy brush he was smoothing over the coat of his favorite mare, Opal. Never mind that he'd been brushing the same spot for nearly ten minutes, caught up in an idle contemplation of the beautiful woman who'd suddenly barged into his home and his life.

How many times that day had he been tempted to wander back to the house, to casually search for a hot cup of coffee or quick snack with the real purpose of seeing her again? According to Jed, she'd spent the entire day yesterday with a tape measure and notepad in hand, scribbling down ideas. And when Jed had begun dinner preparations, she'd swooped down and changed his menu plan, whipping up a deliciously rich Beef Stroganoff to replace the pan-fried steaks his father usually managed to blacken.

That morning at breakfast, she'd blithely prepared another stunning culinary event of scrambled eggs, bacon and homemade biscuits. He'd given her the keys to the truck, expecting her to go right out and buy herself a decent pair of boots—and the ingredients for a gourmet supper that evening. But careful observation of the garage proved that she hadn't left the house at all.

"You don't have to act like you're not listening," Jed muttered, now leaning up against the stall gate. "I've seen the way you look at her."

"And how's that?" Alex asked, unable to ignore the bait.

"Like maybe not every woman in the world is trouble?" his father replied. "Like maybe it's about time to put your problems with Renee in the past?"

Alex bit back a harsh laugh. He'd never put his problems with Renee in the past. Every day he was reminded that he'd failed at marriage and that his son was suffering for that failure. "I made a stupid decision marrying Renee. Hell, we only knew each other for a few months before I asked her to marry me."

"That's the way it always has been for Marrin men," his father said. "We meet the woman of our dreams and it's love at first sight."

"She wasn't the woman of my dreams," Alex muttered. "And neither is Holly Bennett. I won't be making the same mistake twice."

"I don't know. This one's different," Jed said. "She didn't screech and holler when she ended up backside down in a pile of steaming horse apples. Takes a special kind of woman to maintain her composure in the presence of manure."

"She's a city girl. All manners and sophistication. My guess is she can handle herself no matter what might come along."

"Your guess?" Jed scoffed. "It wouldn't hurt you to get to know her. That little girl is working her tail off for your son. She's up at the house right now scurrying around like a squirrel in a nut factory. I've never seen a body get so worked up over Christmas cookies. She's sent me to the store twice today to fetch her ingredients. Says we're havin' cocoa van for dinner. I figure that's some kind of fancy chocolate dessert shaped like a truck.''

"*Coq au vin,*" Alex corrected. "Chicken in wine sauce." His stomach growled in response and he realized that he hadn't bothered with lunch that day.

"Oh, yeah? Well, that's even better."

"It would do you well to remember that you've got work in the barn," Alex said, tossing the dandy brush into the bucket as he grabbed the handle. "Your job doesn't include fetching for her. She can drive herself to the store."

She could do a whole lot more than drive, Alex mused. His thoughts drifted back to that first morning, when he'd carried her in his arms and kissed her bandaged finger. Though the gesture had been instinctive, his reaction hadn't been. In truth, he'd wanted to draw her into his embrace and cover her mouth with his, to see if the taste of a woman was still as powerful as he remembered.

Alex cursed softly. So he'd been a long time without feminine companionship. Hell, it went deeper than that. In his whole life he'd only had a handful of women. He'd met Renee nine years ago, when they were twenty. He'd asked her to marry him three months later. Not much time for sowing wild oats, Alex mused. Maybe that's why he found himself so attracted to Holly. She was a confident and sophisticated woman, she was beautiful, and she was in close proximity. He dropped the bucket on the concrete floor with a clatter. And that's exactly how it had all started with the fickle Renee.

He stepped out of the stall to find his father leaning against a post, a piece of timothy clenched in his teeth, his gaze fixed on Alex. "Don't ruin this for Eric," Jed warned. "Be nice to her or stay away. There's no middle ground here."

Alex shook his head, then stalked to the door, the faint sound of Jed's chuckle echoing through the silent barn. Of course, he'd be nice! He wasn't some rube from up-state New York, some farm boy lacking in manners. He could certainly maintain a cordial relationship with Holly Bennett—and without lapsing into sexual longing every few minutes!

He wasn't prepared for the assault on his senses when he walked in the door. Christmas carols piped cheerily from the stereo in the family room, filling the house with music. The scent of baking was thick in the air and he followed his nose into the kitchen. She'd started a fire in the family room fireplace and the wood snapped and popped. But it was the kitchen that stopped him short.

Every surface, from countertop to table to the top of the refrigerator, was covered with neat rows of cookies, arranged in military precision, each regiment a different variety. Holly, humming along with "Silver Bells," popped up from in front of the oven, a cookie pan in her hand. She froze at the sight of him, their gazes locking for a brief moment, before she smiled and set the pan down. "Hi," she murmured.

"What's all this?" Alex asked.

"I've just been doing a little baking. I had your father run to the store for some staples—flour, butter, eggs, chocolate."

Alex's brow quirked up, amused by her penchant for understatement. "A little baking? We could keep a small third world country in cookies for a year."

Holly glanced around the room, as if she'd just realized how many cookies she'd baked. "Right. I—I guess I did get a little carried away. But you have to have variety. One or two different cookies on a plate doesn't look nearly as festive as ten or twelve. Here, let me show you.''

She snatched a plate from the cupboard and artfully arranged a selection of cookies. Then she ladled a fragrant liquid from the battered crockpot into a mug and dropped in a cinnamon stick. ''Mulled cider,'' she said. She placed the plate of cookies and the mug in front of him, then crossed her arms. ''Go ahead. Try it. The cider is a perfect accompaniment for the butter cookies.''

She watched him intently and he slowly reached for a cookie.

''No!'' she cried.

Alex pulled his fingers away. ''No?''

''Try that one first,'' Holly said. ''And then that one. The pecan shortbread is an acquired taste. More of a tea cookie. Not as sweet as the others.''

He took a butter cookie filled with jam and coated with toasted coconut, then popped it into his mouth. He was prepared to offer lavish compliments, knowing that Holly would be shattered if he just swallowed it and nodded in approval. But Alex stifled a soft moan as the impossibly fresh cookie simply melted on his tongue. He had to admit that he'd never tasted anything quite so good. Cheap store-bought cookies had been the norm in the Marrin household for years and since no one bothered to close the bag, they were usually stale after the first day.

''I'm going to make some gift boxes for them,'' she said, turning back to the pan of cookies on the stove. ''Eric and I can use some Christmas ink stamps to decorate them and then we'll line them with cellophane and gold foil and tie them with a pretty ribbon and—''

''Why?'' Alex asked, surreptitiously snatching a handful of cookies and dropping them into his jacket pocket.

"You could have bought cookies. It wouldn't have made any difference to us."

"That's not the point," Holly said, clearly stunned by his obtuse views on the matter. "You can't give friends and relatives store-bought cookies! It's—it's just not done."

"Wait a second. We're giving all these cookies away?" He grabbed two more handfuls and managed to hide them in his pockets before she turned around.

"With all the friends and relatives that stop by over the—"

Alex cleared his throat, after downing another cookie. "Ah, there won't be any friends," he said, his mouth full. "No relatives, either."

"You don't have any company? But it's Christmas!" Holly cried. "Everyone has company at Christmas!"

He shrugged. "We live a pretty quiet life here."

"But—but—what are we going to do with all these cookies?" She studied the countertop, then smiled. "What about the feed store? And Eric's teachers? And his bus driver?"

He grinned, then snatched up another handful of the pretty little butter cookies with jam in the center. "And we can have cookies for supper. And they're great for breakfast. And lunch. For a guy who usually eats toast two out of three meals, cookies are like gourmet fare."

"Speaking of dinner," Holly said. "I was hoping to take Eric out shopping tonight after we eat. We need to buy decorations for the house. I thought we'd start at Dalton's and look for Christmas tree ornaments. Would that be all right?"

Alex circled the counter, examining another variety of cookie. Holly watched him, her wavy hair tumbled around her face, streaks of flour caught in the strands and smudged on her cheeks. He stood next to her and looked down into her eyes. Lord, she was pretty. "As long as he finishes his homework, he can go," Alex murmured, his gaze skimming over her features.

"I—I used to make these cookies with my mother," Holly explained, turning back to her work. "Every Christmas. I know all these recipes by heart." She picked up a frosted Christmas tree and took a delicate bite. "The taste brings back so many memories." A wistful look crossed her face. "It's funny the things you remember from childhood. "

Alex sighed. "Maybe that's why Eric wrote the letter. He's looking for a few memories." He drew a deep breath. "I should thank you," he said.

She glanced up, her eyes questioning. "For what?"

"For all this. For taking the time." He reached out and gently wiped the smudge of flour from her face, letting his thumb brush across her silken skin. But he couldn't bring himself to break the contact, an undeniable attraction drawing them ever closer. Alex bent near, wanting, needing to kiss her.

"Holy cow! Look at this!"

Alex jumped back, startled by the sound of his son's voice. Nervously he raked his hand through his hair, then forced a smile. He expected Eric to be staring at them both, wondering why his father had been contemplating kissing the Christmas angel. But his son's attention had been captured by the cookies. Kenny stood at his side, his own eyes wide with anticipation.

Alex glanced back at Holly and found the color high in her cheeks. Had his son not come in at that very moment, he knew he would have swept her into his arms. How would he have explained such a sight to Eric? Good grief, the last thing he wanted to do was confuse Eric with adult matters. Holly Bennett was here for only two weeks. He had no intention of making her a permanent fixture at Stony Creek Farm.

"I need to get back to the barn," he murmured, grabbing his mug of cider. He circled around the counter, then ruffled Eric's hair. "Holly is going to take you shopping tonight, Scout. You can go as soon as you get your homework done."

"Wait!" Holly cried. "You can't leave yet. We need to discuss all my plans."

"Dad!" Eric groaned. "You have to discuss her plans!"

"With just two weeks, we'll have to adhere to a strict schedule," Holly began. "And I'll need you to approve my ideas for the interior and exteriors. And as I said before, I've decided to use a rustic theme, which is something I've—"

"I'm sure anything you suggest will be fine," Alex said. "If Eric likes it, I will, too."

He hurried out, anxious to put some space between them. The door clicked shut behind him and he started back toward the barn, ready for a few more hours of hard work. But halfway there, he found himself craving another cookie. He reached in his pocket and found a pretty checkerboard cookie, then popped it into his mouth. But it didn't satisfy him. Alex raked his fingers through his hair. Maybe it was the baker and not the baked goods he was really craving. Unfortunately that was a craving he'd have to learn to ignore.

HOLLY STARED OUT the frosty window of the pickup truck as it bumped along the road leading to downtown Schuyler Falls. Snowflakes, caught in the headlights, danced on the road in front of them. On her right, Eric sat, his eyes wide with excitement, his little body squirming against the seat belt. She'd never met a child quite so sweet and kind as Eric Marrin. His enthusiasm for the season seemed to spill over on to her, making her look forward to every minute leading up to Christmas Eve.

She risked a glance to her left, at Alex, who sat behind the wheel of the truck, silent, stoic, his strong, capable hands wrapped around the wheel, keeping the truck safe on the slick road. Holly hadn't planned to invite Alex along. After their encounter in the kitchen that afternoon, any contact with him was fraught with peril. Instead of thinking about cookie recipes and menu plans, she always seemed to lapse into a contemplation of Alex's broad shoulders or his stunning features or his long, muscular legs. Or his lips, those hard, chiseled, tempting lips. Even now, she couldn't help but sneak a few long looks at him under cover of the dim interior of the truck.

She shouldn't have invited him, but once she learned the truck didn't have an automatic transmission, she'd had no choice. He'd agreed grudgingly, grumbling that he'd never finish all his work in the barn after an evening wasted with shopping. But she knew enough to require only a ride to and from Dalton's. Taking a man—especially a man as stubborn and moody as Alex—through the front doors of a department store could be a disaster of biblical proportions. Men just didn't appreciate the sheer joy of a good retail experience.

"How about some music?" Holly suggested, reaching over to flip on the radio. A blare of Aerosmith split the air behind her head and she jumped, pressing her hand to her chest. A tiny smile quirked the corners of his mouth at her reaction. She quickly found some Christmas music and, before long, she was humming softly along with Miss Piggy and the Muppets in a rousing rendition of "The

Twelve Days of Christmas.'' Both Eric and Alex stared at her as if she'd suddenly gone mad.

"You know, in times past, Christmas was celebrated over a twelve-day period," Holly said. "This Christmas carol is nearly three hundred years old and it's steeped in tradition. Back then, people gave gifts on each of the twelve days."

"You don't say," Alex muttered.

"Twelve days of gifts?" Eric gasped.

"I've been thinking of decorating the living room with a Twelve Days' theme." She stole a glance at Alex, hoping that he'd offer at least one opinion on her decorating ideas. Was he completely bereft of Christmas spirit? And good taste?

"Can we get reindeer?" Eric asked. "Big plastic reindeer with lights inside like Kenny has at his house? Dad, you could put them up on the roof."

Holly winced inwardly. Reindeer were fine for shopping malls but a bit too tacky for such a pretty setting as Stony Creek Farm. "Perhaps we could find something a little less—"

"Now there's an idea I like," Alex said, barely able to suppress a teasing grin. "The more stuff on the roof, the better. And we've got all that space on the lawn, too. And along the driveway and around the barns. We could make it look just like…Vegas in the Adirondacks!"

"Yeah!" Eric cried. "Just like Vegas!" He leaned over to look at his father. "What's Vegas?"

"It's a place where bad Christmas decorators go to die," Holly said, shooting Alex an impatient glare. She turned to Eric. "I don't think we're going to find plastic reindeer at Dalton's."

"Dalton's has everything," Eric said. "Raymond has lights on his tree that look like bugs! You get lots of 'em and it looks like the tree is crawlin' with bugs. His mom got them at Dalton's. Can we get some of those lights?''

Holly swallowed hard. "Bugs?"

"Oh, I think a bug tree would be perfect," Alex said. "How does the song go? Twelve crickets chirping, eleven spiders crawling, ten worms a-wiggling."

Holly glanced over at him and caught him staring at her, his eyes bright, his jaw twitching with humor. "I thought you didn't want anything to do with my plans." Their gazes locked for a moment and Holly felt her breath catch in her throat. Though at first his expression seemed benign, when she looked into his eyes she saw something there, intense, magnetic, almost predatory. She quickly looked away, hoping that he couldn't see the flush heating her cheeks.

"Eric wants the bugs," he said with a grin.

He really was a handsome man when he smiled. Strong and vital, and oh-so sexy. At times so serious and then downright silly. What woman in her right mind would choose to leave a man like Alex Marrin?

"I can work with bugs," she murmured, outvoted two to one. "I'm flexible." Though Holly preferred to do things her own way to insure that everything fit in with an overall theme, she'd done a few bizarre themes in the past. A trout fishing tree for a dyed-in-the-wool sportsman and a tree decorated with little plastic internal organs for a doctor's home. She gnawed on her lower lip. Horses probably had bugs of some sort, horse cooties. She could work it in.

As she mulled over her plans, her gaze dropped to her leg, to the spot where it pressed against Alex's thigh in the cramped confines of the truck. Even through her coat, she could feel his warmth, warmth that slowly seeped through her bloodstream until the chill had been banished from her fingers and toes. How easy it would be to reach over and run her palm along the faded fabric of his jeans, to feel the hard muscle and warm flesh beneath. To let it slide higher and higher until—

She gulped convulsively. "We'll have to have two trees," Holly said. "A very nice formal tree in the living room and a...a bug tree in the family room. And the library could use a tree, too."

"Cool," Eric said. "We never had three trees before! Santa's gonna love our house."

Holly turned to Alex but his gaze was fixed on the street ahead. The pretty homes had given way to businesses as they approached the town square. A few minutes later, the truck pulled up in front of Dalton's Department Store. "I'll pick you up in three hours," Alex said. He reached behind Holly and gave Eric's head a tousle. "Be good for Miss Bennett, Scout. Stay right with her and don't wander off."

He turned his attention to Holly and she wondered when he'd remove his arm from around her shoulders. He was so close she could feel the warmth of his breath on her cold cheek. She let her head tip back slightly, amazed at how perfectly her nape felt in the crook of his arm. "Maybe you could buy some new clothes," he suggested. "And a sturdy pair of boots while you're at it."

He pulled his arm out from around her shoulders. Holly forced a smile, then slid across the seat and hopped out of the truck right after Eric. Before she could say another word to Alex, Eric grabbed her hand and dragged her to the wide glass windows, pushing through the crowds that had gathered there.

"Look at the trains!" he cried, pressing his face against the glass like the rest of the kids lining the windows. He drew her to the next window. "And these bears play in a band! See how they move?"

As Eric pulled her to the next window, she glanced over her shoulder and found Alex watching them. He'd stepped out of the truck and now stood with his arms braced on the hood, his gaze following them both. From this distance, she couldn't read his expression, only that he wasn't smiling. For such a seemingly unaffected man, he was endlessly complicated, his mood shifting in the blink of an eye.

When she looked for him again a moment later, the truck was gone and Holly felt strangely disappointed. It had been so long since a man had looked at her with anything more than mild interest. And so long since she'd even bothered to care. With a soft laugh, she pulled Eric away from the windows. "Come on, we have shopping to do!"

They hurried through the revolving door, then stopped inside the grand entryway of Dalton's. Holly felt as if she'd been instantly transported back in time. This was the way shopping used to be, with smiling salesclerks who called you by name and uniformed doormen who welcomed you with a nod. The terrazzo floors shone and the smell of lemon oil drifted off the rich mahogany paneling.

As they strolled past the perfume counter, she noticed the huge Christmas tree set in the center of the store. Slowly her eyes rose, higher and higher, up through a soaring atrium three stories high. Above her, shoppers rested along the railings, staring out at the twinkling lights and shiny ornaments. A tiny thrill raced through her and, for a moment, she felt like a young girl again, full of the excitement of the season.

"It's magical," Holly murmured. "And a real tree. I wonder how they got it in here?"

"They always have a big tree." Eric pulled her along toward the escalator. "First, we have to go see Santa. Then we can look at the tree."

"I thought you already talked to Santa," Holly said, hurrying to match his pace.

"I have to thank him," Eric said.

"For what?"

"For you!"

Holly's heart warmed at his innocent compliment. She'd only been a Christmas angel for a few days, but she already knew it was the best job she'd ever had. Devoting herself to the happiness of a sweet boy like Eric Marrin could hardly be called work.

They stepped onto the old escalator and ascended to the second floor, then joined the long line of children waiting at the gate to a cute little gingerbread village. The place was lined with aisles of toys, but Eric didn't even notice, his gaze fixed squarely on the entrance to Santa's kingdom.

As they waited, Holly was reminded of her childhood, how resolute she'd been in her own belief in Santa, and how she had challenged anyone who told her differently. Here, with Eric's hand clutching hers, she could almost believe again in the pure magic of Christmas, and the warmth and security of a family to share it with.

"Hey, kid! What are you doing back here?"

They both turned to see one of Santa's elves approaching—Twinkie, by her name tag. Holly felt Eric's hand squeeze hers a little tighter. "Hi, Twinkie! Look what I brought. It's my Christmas angel."

The elf stared down at Eric, her hands braced on her hips. "Your what?"

"My angel. Her name is Holly and Santa sent her to

me. She's going to make my Christmas perfect. I came back here to thank him.''

The elf's gaze rose to Holly's face and she stared at her shrewdly, her pretty features pensive, curious. A bit too curious for Holly's liking. "Santa sent you?" she asked. "That's not true, is it?"

Holly glanced over her shoulder, uneasy with the elf's sudden interest in private matters. "I—I'm really not at liberty to say," she replied. "Come on, Eric, we'll come back a little later and thank Santa. We've got a lot of shopping to do." She tugged on his hand and led him away.

"Wait," the elf cried, weaving through the waiting crowd. "I just have a few questions to ask."

They lost the elf somewhere in bed linens, crouching behind a pile of down comforters to conceal themselves and holding their breaths as Twinkie's jingling elf boots passed by. When Holly was sure they were safe, she pulled Eric to his feet. "Maybe it would be best if we didn't tell anyone else about your Christmas angel," she suggested.

"Why?"

Holly scrambled to come up with a logical reason. "Because we wouldn't want all the other kids to ask for their own angels. There are just so many angels to go around and we wouldn't want anyone to be disappointed."

Eric nodded solemnly. "Yes. Maybe that would be best."

As they searched out the tree trimming department, Holly glanced down at Eric and smoothed his mussed hair. He looked up at her and smiled, his whole face radiating joy. How different he was from his father, Holly mused. While Eric Marrin wore his emotions on his sleeve, his father hid them behind a stony face. While Eric was friendly and outgoing, Alex Marrin was aloof and indifferent.

She sighed softly. She'd stepped into the lives of these two males intending to do her job and make her $15,000. But this was more than a job. It was a chance to make a real difference in Eric's life, to give him something that he'd been missing. If the contract were canceled tomorrow, Holly knew she'd never be able to abandon the job. She was already falling under the spell of the little boy's charm.

She drew a steadying breath. Now, if she could only avoid doing the same with his father.

A FRESH DUSTING OF SNOW had fallen that morning and, in the waning light of day, it sparkled like tiny diamonds. Alex drew a deep breath of the cold afternoon air. As he looked out over the rolling land, the thick trees and wide meadows, he smiled. This was his land, his future—and the future of his son. Nothing could tear him away from this place. Not even a woman.

Renee had tried to draw him away, to force him into her life in New York City. But when he'd insisted they come back to Stony Creek when she got pregnant, she'd had no choice but to agree. From the day she set foot on the farm, he knew she didn't belong. It shouldn't have come as a surprise when she left six years later, but it did.

He glanced back at Holly, who trudged through the snow in his footsteps, Eric at her side. The two of them, bundled against the cold, held hands, Eric staring up at Holly as if she really were an angel sent from above. But to Alex, she'd become a siren sent by the devil himself, sent to torment and tempt him with her beauty and her allure. She didn't belong here, either. Even dressed in insulated boots and a thick wool field jacket, she still looked like a city girl.

He vowed to maintain his distance from her again and again, but at every turn, she was there, asking him questions, seeking out his help. He'd had his resolve sorely tested trying not to touch her while he drove them back from their shopping spree at Dalton's last night. And when she thanked him for carrying her parcels into the house, he'd fought an overwhelming urge to bend a little nearer and kiss her. Even this morning at breakfast, he couldn't seem to keep his eyes off of her, preoccupied with a covert inventory of her pretty features.

And now, even with the cold air and the bright sunshine, he wanted to pull her into his arms and tumble into the snow. Instead he was forced to focus on the task at hand—finding three suitable Christmas trees for the house. He stopped to stare up at a twelve-foot balsam pine, then waited for Holly and Eric to catch up.

"How about this one?" he asked.

Holly's gaze skimmed over the height and width of the tree, then she slowly circled it, taking in its every detail. She'd already rejected the past forty-seven trees he'd shown her and if she rejected another, he'd be hard-pressed not to toss her in the nearest snowbank and continue the search without her.

"I don't know," Holly said. "It seems a little bare on the other side. And it's really not very thick." She sighed. "It would be much more efficient if we just went to a tree lot and bought three trees. We just don't have the time to search."

Alex ground his teeth as he attempted to bite back a sarcastic retort. This is precisely why he didn't shop with women. Whether they were looking for something as complex as panty hose or something as simple as a damn

Christmas tree, they always had to turn it into a major production. "We'll put the bare spot against the wall," he said. "No one will know it's there."

"*I'll* know," Holly said. "And it won't be perfect."

"Nothing I show you is going to be perfect," Alex replied. "It's not supposed to be perfect. The reason we're cutting our own tree is that we always cut our own tree. It's family tradition."

"You don't have to get mad," Holly shouted. "I'll find a tree. It will just take time. Sometimes my father and I would search for days for just the perfect tree."

Alex stopped and slowly turned to Holly. "Days? We've been out here four hours and that's three hours longer than you deserve. It's getting dark, you've seen hundreds of trees. Balsam, white pine, Scotch pine. Ten-feet tall, twelve-feet tall, thick and thin, short needles, long needles. Just tell me what you want!"

"I want something special," Holly said. She crossed her arms over her breasts and stared at him, her nose rosy, her eyes bright. "Perfect."

"Perfect. The only perfect thing you're going to find in this woods is a perfect lunatic with a perfectly honed ax and a perfectly sharpened saw, and a perfectly reasonable reason to murder you if you don't pick out a tree right now!"

She gave him a haughty look, refusing to back down. "If you're going to be so belligerent, why don't you just go back to the house?"

"Belligerent?" Alex asked. "You think this is belligerent?" He reached down and picked up a handful of snow, packing it with his gloved hands.

Holly held out her hand to warn him off. "Don't even think of throwing that at me."

Alex ignored the warning, taking her words as a challenge. When he refused to put the snowball down, Holly scrambled to make her own ammunition, enlisting Eric's help. Alex released a tightly held breath. Though he'd derive great pleasure in giving her a faceful of snow, it wasn't going to get them out of the woods any faster. "All right," he said, tossing his snowball aside. "Truce. But you've got thirty minutes to find a decent trio of trees or I'm going to leave you out here to freeze."

"Hey, Dad, you're a poet and you don't even know it!"

Alex turned on his heel and started down the trail once again. But the shock of cold snow on his bare neck stopped him short. With a low growl, he slowly faced them. They both looked guilty as sin, satisfied smiles pasted on their rosy-cheeked faces. He raised his brow at Eric and his son tipped his head toward Holly.

In one smooth motion, he scooped up a handful of snow, packed it tight and took a step toward her. He was about to show her exactly who wore the pants around Stony Creek Farm. Holly let out a tiny shriek, then spun around and headed for the safety of a small tree.

Eric grabbed up a snowball and threw it at Alex, hitting him on the thigh. Alex scowled at his son. "So that's the way it is. You're going to side with the girl?"

"She's my angel and I have to protect her." He thumped his chest with his fist. "And this is war!" Eric let out a piercing battle cry, then scampered over to Holly's hiding place.

A full-scale battle erupted with Alex taking the brunt of the assault. He tore through the trees, looking for Holly only to get ambushed by another snowball from Eric. And when he took off after Eric, Holly would come to the boy's rescue with a barrage of snowballs meant to lay him low.

Breathless and wet with water running down his neck and settling near the small of his back, Alex decided to employ a new strategy—stealth. He gathered up a handful of snow and tiptoed through the trees, stopping to listen every few seconds. His efforts paid off, for a few moments later, he came up behind Holly.

Slowly he crept toward her as she peered out from behind a squat little fir tree. At the last minute, she heard him and, with a loud yell, Alex grabbed her from behind and playfully wrestled her down into the snow. He caught her wrists in one hand and pinned them above her head. She didn't have time to scream before he washed her face with the snowball. Coughing and sputtering, she looked up at him, her lashes covered with ice crystals.

But the battle between them quickly faded as Alex stared down at her. She lay perfectly still, her slender body stretched beneath his, their hips pressed together. Her breath came in quick, deep gasps, visible in the cold air. And though he refused to let her go, she didn't attempt to shout for Eric's help.

He gently wiped the snow from her eyes. "Do you surrender?" Alex asked, keenly aware of the deeper meaning to his question.

She nodded, her gaze fixed on his, her lips parted. He brushed a strand of hair from her cheek and, to his surprise, she turned her face into his palm, tempting him with a subtle sign of her desire, closing her eyes to await his kiss. Groaning softly, Alex bent nearer, already anticipating the warm sweetness of her mouth, the flood of need that promised to rush through his bloodstream.

But a moment before their lips met, Alex heard a rustling in the nearby trees. He released her wrists and pushed up, bracing his arms on either side of her head.

When Eric's scream split the cold, silent air, Holly stiffened beneath him, then began to wriggle.

Alex groaned. "The kid has impeccable timing."

"Let me up!" she cried.

The electricity between them died instantly, doused by a healthy dose of reality. When Alex saw Eric's boots beneath the trees, he rolled to the side. Holly scrambled to her feet and frantically began to brush the snow from her clothes. "You shouldn't have done that," she murmured, refusing to meet his gaze. "I—I'm here to do a job and nothing more. I trust you'll remember that from now on?"

Alex smiled as he struggled to his feet, evidence of his desire pressing against the snow-dampened fabric of his jeans. "Hey, all's fair in love and war," he replied. "Isn't that what they say?"

She opened her mouth to snap out a reply, but just then Eric appeared from behind the tree. He took in his father's appearance, then grinned. "Holly got you good!" he cried. "We win, we win!"

Alex cleared his throat, then nodded. "Yeah, Scout, Holly got me good."

The "victor" pasted a bright smile on her face and held out her hand to Eric. "We better get going," she said. "We still have three trees to find." Without looking at Alex, she brushed by him and trudged off on her quest for perfection.

When Alex caught up to them, a full five minutes later, he'd managed to quell his physical reaction to their encounter, but couldn't banish the sense of regret he felt. What might have happened if they'd been alone in the woods, without interruption? Would they have given in to their attraction, finally and fully? She'd wanted him to kiss her. He'd seen it in her eyes, in the way her mouth quivered slightly, in the soft clouds of frozen breath that betrayed her excitement. But how much longer could they both deny what was so blatantly obvious? They wanted each other, in the simplest, most primal way.

"Come on, Dad!" Eric called. "Holly found a tree she likes."

She stood beside a balsam that resembled every other balsam she'd rejected, her hands clutched in front of her, her attention firmly on the tree. "This is the one," she murmured, again refusing to look at him.

Alex circled the tree, knowing full well that she'd chosen the first thing she'd come upon. It was clear she'd do anything to escape his presence, including settling for a substandard tree. "What about this bare spot?" he asked.

"We can put it against the wall," she said, her earlier enthusiasm diminished, her expression uneasy. "And that little one, over there, will be fine for the library. And the one over there for the family room. If you'll just cut them down, we can be on our way."

She was upset, but Alex wasn't sure why. Could he have misread her reactions? Had he been so long without a woman that he couldn't tell the difference between desire and distaste? He cursed inwardly, cursed his runaway urges and his unbidden reaction to them. "Eric, why don't you take Miss Bennett back to the house. She looks a little…cold."

That brought a response, narrowed eyes and cheeks stained red from more than just the frigid air. "I can find my way back on my own," she said defensively.

"I'm sure you can. But I'd feel better if Eric showed you the way. He knows this land as well as I do."

Alex watched them go, standing in the same spot until they disappeared behind a low rise in the landscape. Then with a soft groan, he sat down in the snow. Though he'd tried his best to resist her, there was no denying the truth. He wasn't going to be satisfied until he kissed Holly Bennett, long and hard and deep. Maybe then, he'd be able to put this strange fascination behind him. That was the answer, then. At the next available opportunity, he'd pull her into his arms and kiss her. And finally, that would be the end of it.

Or maybe, it would just be a beginning.

4

THE FLAMES IN THE fireplace had ebbed to glowing embers by the time Holly finished decorating Eric's tree in the family room. He'd grown bored with hanging ornaments and was now fast asleep on the sofa, his head nestled against Thurston's stomach. Though Alex appeared to be absorbed in the newspaper, Holly felt his gaze on her every time she turned her back, making the hairs on her arms prickle and tingle.

How had things moved so quickly between them? Just three nights ago, she was standing on his front porch, a complete stranger, and now they were lusting after each other like love-starved teenagers. Though she'd tried to control her impulses in his presence, she always seemed to forget herself, to ignore the woman she was supposed to be.

Holly had never put much stock in passion. She and Stephan had shared a satisfying relationship in bed, but it had never been fireworks and angel choirs. But then, she'd never expected that, so how could she have known what she was missing?

Now she did. That little flutter that leaped in her stomach every time she looked at Alex. The ache she felt deep in her core every time he brushed against her. The look she saw in his eyes when he meant to kiss her. She'd come to crave them all.

Her head warned her to keep her relationship with Alex

strictly business. But her heart said there was more than just business between them. After their tumble in the snow, she could think of nothing more than finishing what they'd started, giving in to the kiss that hadn't happened. But where would a simple kiss lead? The only path Holly could see was the path to a broken heart and she was determined to avoid that route.

She placed the last ornament on the tree, then stepped back. Though she hadn't been completely sold on the idea of a "bug" tree, she had to admit the nature theme worked well. They'd added bird ornaments to the lady-bugs and butterflies and bees, along with Eric's dragonfly lights. Holly had found natural garland made of tiny pine-cones and dried wildflowers to emphasize the backyard garden theme. Though it wasn't her most sophisticated tree, it had its charms. "What do you think?" she murmured, staring up at the birdhouse that topped the tree.

"Pardon?"

Holly tweaked one of Eric's dragonfly lights, then turned around. "What do you think?"

Alex glanced down at Eric. "I think I'd better put this guy to bed." He set his newspaper down, then reached out to slip his arm beneath his son. The little boy opened his eyes and yawned.

When he caught sight of the tree, ablaze with the twinkling dragonflies, he smiled sleepily. "Cool," he murmured. He pushed up from the sofa and crossed the room. Wrapping his arms around Holly's waist, he gave her a hug, warming Holly's heart. "See you in the morning, Holly."

She patted his head, then watched as he returned to his father's side. They both walked out of the room, leaving her with a tiny smile on her lips. The love between father and son was so apparent, so assured that she felt the power

of it just being near them. She'd shared the same security
with her own father, the unfaltering bond between parent
and child. Someday, she'd have that for herself, a child
to love her unconditionally.

But when she conjured herself a family, the picture was
no longer vague and unfocused. Eric was the child she
pictured as her own. And Alex Marrin had taken over the
role as fantasy father and perfect mate. Not that she
wanted to marry *him* and have *his* children. But she
wanted a father for her children who could love as deeply
as he did.

Holly sighed softly, then began to gather the boxes and
bags scattered around the floor. When she'd tidied the
room, she walked over to the light switch and flipped the
lights off. This was always her favorite moment, when the
tree came to life in front of her eyes. She wasn't sure how
long she stared at the tree, enjoying the pungent odor of
fresh pine and the soft light thrown across the ceiling.

"Beautiful."

She turned to find Alex standing a few feet behind her.
"You like it?"

"I wasn't talking about the tree."

Holly felt a blush warm her cheeks. How a simple compliment could disarm her! Especially when it came from
Alex Marrin. "I think the bugs work."

"Would you like a glass of wine?" Alex asked.

Holly nearly caught herself accepting his offer. "Now
that I've finished here, I should get to work hanging the
garland in the library. And I've got to plan for the—"

He took her arms and slowly turned her around. Without hesitation, he cupped her face between his hands and
brought his lips softly down on hers. The kiss was so
gentle, so unexpected, that Holly wasn't sure what to do.

No surge of indignation washed over her, no embarrassment or guilt. Just warm and wonderful pleasure.

His mouth lingered over hers for a long time, testing, tasting. Holly slid her palms up his chest and wrapped her arms around his neck, sinking against him. When he tried to pull back, she urged him not to stop, her fingers splayed across his nape. A soft moan rumbled low in his throat as the passion grew between them by degrees.

"I've been wanting to do this since that very first night," he murmured, his breath soft against her cheek. He traced a line of kisses from her jaw to the notch at the base of her neck. "Tell me you wanted this, too."

"I—I'm not sure," Holly murmured, tipping her head back to fully enjoy the feel of his mouth on her skin. She thought she knew exactly what she wanted, to maintain a safe distance from Alex. But now, she found herself wanting his kisses much more.

Alex furrowed his hand through her hair, then forced her to meet his gaze. "Why do you deny this? We're attracted to each other, Holly. It's really quite simple."

"But it's not," she said. "I'm here to do a job. And I have a life back in New York City, a career and business to run."

He arched his brow. "I'm not asking you to stay," Alex murmured. "This isn't a proposal of marriage."

Holly drew in a sharp breath, the warmth his kiss had brought leaving her body. She placed her palms on his chest and pushed him away. "Which is exactly why we can't do this," she said.

"You want an engagement ring before you'll let me kiss you again?"

"No!" Holly cried. "Don't be ridiculous."

"Then what is it?"

She scrambled for a sane reason why she couldn't allow herself to be seduced by Alex Marrin's charm. But nothing she came up with made the least bit of sense. Why not kiss him, as long as it felt good? Why not let passion take its course? It's not as if she were engaged to Stephan! She was a single woman, free to explore her passions with whatever man she chose. "There's another man," she blurted out, taking the first excuse she could find.

Alex nuzzled her neck playfully. "There won't be after tonight."

"It's quite serious." She felt his lips abandon the pulse point on her neck. His shoulders stiffened and he drew away.

"You're engaged?" He stared at her as if she'd suddenly sprouted horns and a pitchfork tail.

The emotion in his eyes, barely controlled anger, self-loathing, made her retreat a step. "No. I—I mean, yes. We've known each other for ages and last Christmas Stephan asked me to marry him." It wasn't really a lie, just not the entire truth.

"I don't see an engagement ring," Alex said.

"I don't need a ring to remind me of how I feel."

"And how do you feel when you're with him, Holly?" Alex asked. "Does he make you feel the way I do? All warm and breathless? Out of control? Willing to do anything for this?" He caught her around the waist and yanked her closer.

"Stop it," she warned, her gaze transfixed by the desire blazing in his eyes, her voice lacking any conviction.

He leaned closer. "Make me." With that, he lowered his mouth to hers. She expected all the anger she saw in his expression to flow into his kiss. But it wasn't there. Only need, desire so fierce that she could feel it flooding into her body from his. And when he drew away, leaving her breathless, her instinct was only to lash back at him for taking away every ounce of her self-control.

"You can't change the past by punishing me. I'm not her, Alex, and when I leave after Christmas and all the decorations are put away and all the cookies are eaten, you won't be able to blame me. I won't be abandoning you. I'll just be going back to my life."

He cursed softly, then turned away from her. The heat from his body suddenly disappeared and Holly shivered. "Well, I guess that answers all my questions," he said. He rubbed his hands together, then glanced around the room. "Do you need any help cleaning up here? If not, I've got work to do in the barn."

"That's it?" Holly asked.

He forced a smile. "Don't worry, Miss Bennett. I won't be kissing you anytime soon. Unless, of course, you beg me to." With that, he grabbed his jacket and strode to the back door.

The sharp sound of it slamming made her jump and she pressed her palm to her chest, only to find her heart beating like an overwound clock. "Good," she murmured, "I'm glad that's all cleared up." She took in a shaky breath, then turned to finish tidying up the family room. But her body trembled so uncontrollably that she finally had to sit down.

This was good, wasn't it? Alex didn't want her anymore. No more lustful looks, no more passionate longing. No more kisses? Holly groaned and put her face in her hands. Now, if she could just convince herself that this was what *she* wanted, she might be able to concentrate on the job at hand. And not on the breathless, reckless, wanton way Alex Marrin made her feel.

"GET PACKED AND TAKE the first train up here," Holly ordered, trying to keep the edge of hysteria from her voice. "There's a train at 8:20 that arrives here just before noon."

"Mom?"

"No! It's Holly."

For a long moment, there was no sound on the other end of the line. Then a groan and a dramatic yawn from Meg. "Holly? It's five in the morning!"

"I know what time it is," Holly said, pacing back and forth alongside her bed. "I want you up here today. At the latest, tomorrow morning. You're taking over this assignment."

Meg's astonished gasp was audible through the phone lines, but that didn't sway Holly. She'd spent a sleepless night scarfing down Christmas cookies and weighing the consequences of remaining at Stony Creek Farm. While waiting for the sun to rise, she'd decided that leaving was the only option she had. Even though Alex had vowed to keep his distance, Holly was convinced, sooner or later, she'd go begging. And when she did, it wouldn't be for mere kisses. No, she'd want more from Alex Marrin.

Her mind wandered back to the kiss they'd shared, the unbridled desire he'd ignited inside her. The moment his lips had touched hers, Holly knew she wanted him. But a tiny corner of her brain blared out a warning she couldn't ignore. She'd known Alex for less than a week and she was ready to toss aside her inhibitions!

How could she possibly know what she wanted? It had taken her almost a year to decide she wanted Stephan and look how badly that turned out! No, Holly Bennett never made spur-of-the-moment decisions. She always weighed all her options carefully, made a plan, considered every angle.

Though an affair with Alex could be wonderfully exciting, it was also a dangerous proposition. She already knew he wasn't the type of man to give his heart freely. His divorce had obviously left scars, deep and painful. And he'd already made his feelings quite clear. He was attracted to her, but there'd be no proposals of marriage, no happily ever after. Whatever she might imagine between them, it would only be sex to him.

"What's this all about?" Meg asked, her voice ragged with sleep.

"I just think you'd be better suited to this assignment."

"Why?"

"Well, you're much—" Holly searched for a plausible reason "—much stronger than I am."

"If there's heavy lifting to be done, why don't you hire someone?" Meg suggested. "We certainly have the budget."

"That's not what I mean," Holly said, dragging her overnight bag from beneath the bed.

Meg paused. "What *do* you mean? Has something happened? You sound upset."

"I'm fine," she said, throwing the bag open.

"You're lying," Meg countered. "I can always tell when you're lying, even over the phone. What's up?"

Holly paused, wondering if she should tell Meg the entire story or just the bare facts. "All right. There's this man. Actually, Eric Marrin's father, Alex. And we have a—a thing between us."

"A thing? Did you get all prissy with him? You know how men hate that. I'm always telling you, you have to be more flexible and more—"

"I wasn't prissy!" She sat down on the edge of the bed. "Just the opposite. Whenever I'm around him, we end up kissing. Or almost kissing."

"You kissed a man?" Meg took a moment to digest

the startling news. "You kissed a man! We are talking about on the lips, aren't we?"

"Once. He almost kissed me in the snow and in the kitchen. And then, there was the time he kissed my finger, but that doesn't count."

"It doesn't?" Meg asked.

"Well, I don't think kissing a girl's hurt finger can qualify as a sexual overture."

"Honey, just because I haven't had a date in six months, doesn't mean *you* can't enjoy yourself."

"I have a reputation to protect," Holly replied.

"Now you *are* being prissy."

"I can't allow myself to have personal feelings for a client." She held her breath, hoping that Meg wouldn't realize that Alex Marrin wasn't exactly a client. Since he wasn't footing the bill for her time and effort, then she was completely free to strip naked and dance around his kitchen in her apron and oven mitts if she felt so inclined. "Please, Meg, you have to help me. If I stay here, I'm not sure what I'll do."

"Gee, you might just go crazy and make wild, passionate love to the guy. And that might be exactly what you need!" Meg cried. "Holly, you have your life so perfectly planned right down to the underwear you're going to wear next Thursday. Maybe it's time you tried a little spontaneity."

"This is not about my character flaws, Meg! This is about sex! Sex with a man who's probably really, *really* good at it. Needless to say, I'm very bad at it. Now, if you want to be hanging tinsel with me next Christmas, you better pack your bags and take the first train north."

"I've got work to finish here," Meg protested. "The soonest I can get on a train is tomorrow morning."

Holly wasn't in the mood to argue any longer. It would

require her to convince Meg that her business reputation was more precious to her than a few nights of torrid sex with Alex Marrin. And right now, even she knew that would be a lie.

She gave Meg a few more instructions, listened to a recitation of her phone messages, then hung up, placing the phone softly in the cradle. With a quiet moan, Holly buried her face in her hands and flopped back onto the bed. How could she have made such a mess of this all? Perhaps if she'd just been firm that first time he almost kissed her.

But it went back farther than that. From the moment they'd met in the horse barn, she felt it. A force drawing them together, magnetic, powerful and completely uncontrollable. As if all her carefully cultivated reserve had suddenly vanished, Holly felt like a woman driven by impulse rather than good common sense.

Rolling over on her stomach, she grabbed the phone book from the bedside table and flipped through it, looking for a cab company, desperate to do something sensible. Though the train didn't leave until that afternoon, the sooner she made her escape, the easier it would be on all of them.

The owner of Schuyler Falls' only cab company answered after seven or eight rings and sounded as if he'd just crawled out of bed. She made arrangements for him to pick her up at the end of the driveway in a half hour. That would give her enough time to finish packing and write a quick note to Eric explaining her sudden departure.

When she had finally stuffed the last bit of clothing into her suitcase, she quickly snapped it shut then grabbed her coat. Holly took one last look around the room, then walked out of the tack house. The sun wasn't even up, but the yard lights lit the way up to the house. She hurried across the porch, eager to avoid the barns, also brightly blazing with light.

But as she turned the corner on the tack house porch, she ran face first into a lean, hard, finely muscled chest, clothed in a familiar canvas jacket. Her bag slipped out of her hand and landed squarely on the toe of her shoe. Holly yelped in pain, then hopped around on one foot. When the pain subsided, she managed to look up into Alex's face.

His eyes darted to her bag. "What's this?" he asked with a frown.

Wincing with pain, Holly snatched up her suitcase and moved around him. "I'm leaving," she said, limping as fast as she could.

"Today?"

"You can finish the other trees and put up the garland around the door and the mantels. You only wanted me to stay for three days and I did."

He fell into step beside her as she started down the porch steps. "That was then," he said. "We discussed this and I told you I—"

"It doesn't make a difference. I think it would be best if I left. I've called my assistant, Meghan O'Malley. She'll be arriving here tomorrow to tie up any loose ends."

"But Eric wants *you*," Alex said, placing his hand on her elbow. "You're his Christmas angel." He drew a long breath, then sighed. "This isn't because I kissed you, is it?"

Holly laughed dryly, ignoring the tiny tremor that raced through her body as his fingers clutched her arm. "Don't flatter yourself," she lied. She pulled out of his grasp, but as soon as her foot hit the walk, it skidded out from under her. She bumped down onto the icy walk, rebruising her already bruised backside.

What was it with this place? When Alex wasn't sweeping her off her feet and kissing her, she managed to sweep herself off her own feet at every turn! Intent on putting some distance between them, she struggled to stand. "I don't want to be anyone's angel," she said.

Alex reached out to help her up, but she slapped his hand away, knowing precisely what his touch could do to her. She brushed the snow off the back of her coat, then hoisted up her bag again and set off at a quicker pace. This time he didn't bother to follow her. "Eric will like Meg. She's really much better with children than I am."

"You're pretty damn good with kids yourself."

Holly stopped, stunned by the unsolicited compliment. She slowly turned to find him staring at her, his gaze fierce, unwavering. "Do you really think so?" she asked.

His expression softened. "Don't go. Eric will miss you. I don't want him to pay for my mistakes."

"Then you admit kissing me was a mistake?" Holly asked, not really ready to hear his answer.

"No. That's not what I meant."

"What is it you want from me?"

Alex's jaw tightened and he shook his head, his mood darkening in the blink of an eye. "Am I supposed to know? I don't know how I feel about you, Holly. Or what I want. I don't think you do, either. But we're never going to find out if you run back to New York like some scared little rabbit."

"I came here to do a job," she said. "But I can't do my job if you're trying to kiss me at every turn."

"And you feel like you're betraying your fiancé?"

Holly frowned. "My fian—oh, yes. My fiancé. That's exactly how I feel," she murmured, nearly forgetting the lie she'd told him the night before.

"An engaged woman doesn't just go around kissing other men," he said.

Holly gasped. "I—I don't kiss at all! You're the one who kissed *me*. And you don't kiss like a gentleman!"

A sardonic grin touched his lips. "I'll take that as a compliment."

"Exactly my point. You are no gentleman." She spun on her heel and started back down the walk, this time avoiding the icy patches. But her progress was stopped when his hand grasped her arm. To fend him off, she swung her suitcase at him. But in her haste to pack, she'd neglected to secure the latches firmly and it flew open, sending her clothes flying over the snow.

Lacy black panties fell at his feet and he bent down to pick them up. He held them out, hooked on one finger and when she reached for them, he snatched them away. "You accuse me of being no gentleman. I'd say these prove you're not the lady you claim to be."

Holly glared at him, her anger bubbling inside. But beneath the anger, there was something else, something more powerful. An impulse, an urge to walk right up to him and kiss him again, to prove what he already knew. To make him feel exactly the way he made her feel. She took a step toward him, grabbed his face between her hands and gave him a punishing kiss, her tongue invading his mouth, her teeth grazing his lower lip. When she was quite positive she'd gotten the desired reaction, she stepped back and shrugged nonchalantly. "Keep the panties then. You can use them to decorate the other Christmas tree."

With that, she turned on her heel, leaving her possessions scattered in the snow. Her heart threatened to pound right out of her chest, and for a moment, she felt a little dizzy. Though it wasn't the most dignified of exits, it would have to do. Because Holly Bennett was through feeling anything at all—including uncontrollable desire—for Alex Marrin. And that kiss proved it!

THE FIRST TRAIN BACK to New York that day was scheduled to leave Schuyler Falls at three o'clock in the afternoon. Since Kenny hung around the train station a lot, he knew all the schedules by heart, even all the stops between home and New York City. Eric had rushed from the bus stop a half block away, hoping and praying that his watch was a few minutes slow. He paused outside the doors with Kenny to catch his breath, just as the speaker above their heads crackled.

"Ladies and gentlemen, passengers with tickets for the three o'clock train to New York City's Penn Station, with stops in Saratoga Springs, Schenectady, Albany, Hudson, Poughkeepsie, and Yonkers, may begin boarding on track one."

"We're too late!" he cried.

"Naw," Kenny replied. "They always board fifteen minutes before the train leaves."

Eric yanked the door open, clutching the special gifts he was carrying, then raced inside. But a quick search of the waiting area found no sign of his Christmas angel. He caught sight of the conductor standing at the door to the tracks. He'd come to meet his mom at the train a few times when she visited, so he knew he could get out on the platform to look for Holly. But what if she'd already boarded?

"Just be cool," Kenny said. "Act casual, like we're going to get on the train." They pulled their hoods up, like the guys in the spy movies did, then strolled outside to the platform.

"I can't see anything! The windows are all dark!" Eric cried.

Kenny shrugged. "Then you're just going to have to go on board. You won't need a ticket. Just tell 'em your mom already got on while you were in the can."

Eric's heart beat at a lickety-split speed and he felt as if he might lose the lunch he'd eaten at Kenny's house. He slowly gathered his courage. This was his angel and he'd do anything to keep her! When he got close enough to the car's steps, he nearly turned back. But the conductor spoke first, startling Eric.

"Are your folks on the train already, boys?" the conductor asked.

"No!" Eric said at the same time Kenny said, "Yes!"

"His mom is," Kenny said. "I'm just here to say good-bye."

Eric gave Kenny the elbow. Though he was a good liar, he was a real chicken when it came to the hard stuff, like getting on a train without a ticket. Eric nodded in agreement. Though he usually tried not to lie, this was important. If he didn't say yes out loud, maybe it wouldn't be such a big lie.

"Go on, then. Hop aboard."

He couldn't believe his luck! The guy was just letting him walk onto the train! Without a ticket, even. He gave Kenny one last look, then scrambled up the steps and walked into the car on his left. He found Holly just a few seats away. She sat with her head against the back of the seat, her eyes closed.

"You can't leave," he said as he plopped down in the seat next to her. When she opened her eyes, Eric shoved a fistful of plastic flowers under her nose, then followed it with a Snickers bar. He'd found the flowers in Kenny's garage and the Snickers was left over from lunch. But it was the best he could do.

"Eric! What are you doing here?" Holly asked, straightening in her seat.

"I came to bring you back," he said. "I don't know why you're mad at me, but—"

She smiled in that soft way that she always did, the way that made him feel all safe inside. "Oh, Eric, I'm not mad at you. I just have some important business in the city."

"Well, if you are mad, I brought you flowers and candy. Kenny says his dad is always bringing his mom flowers and candy when she's mad and it makes it all better."

"How did you get here?" Holly asked.

"I took the bus. Kenny knows all the schedules. He's like a genius when it comes to buses and trains."

"Then you got my letter?"

"I wanted to come and get you this morning, but Dad told me no. So I went over to Kenny's to play and then we just kind of walked to the bus stop and here I am. Kenny's outside." Eric leaned over Holly's lap and pounded on the window, then waved at Kenny. He glanced around the train car. "You know, they don't even ask for your ticket when you get on the train."

"You have to get off," Holly said. "Before the train leaves the station."

He shook his head. "Nope. I'm going to New York with you. I'm going to have Christmas at your house."

He could imagine what Christmas was like at Holly's house. She'd have a huge tree with billions of presents underneath, all wrapped up in paper and ribbons until no one could guess what was inside. She'd have a special plate and cup to leave out for Santa, one with his name on it. She'd let him get up as early as he wanted on Christmas morning. And after he opened all his presents, she'd make waffles with chocolate chips and bacon fried crispy. And fresh squeezed orange juice without the schnibbles.

"What about your dad? And Kenny's parents? They'll be worried about you."

"Kenny knows where I'm going. He'll tell Dad and Gramps. When do we leave? Can we go sit in the car with the glass top?"

Holly groaned, then grabbed Eric by the hand. "You're not going anywhere. And I guess I'm not, either. We're going to get off this train and I'm going to take you home before your dad misses *you* and blames *me*."

Eric grinned and jumped up from his seat. "I knew I could get you back. So what was it? The candy or the flowers?"

She climbed down the steps, then reached back for Eric and swung him down behind her. "It was that smile of yours," she said, tweaking his nose. "You're a very charming young man."

"He doesn't take after his father."

The sound of his father's voice sent a shiver of regret through Eric's body. He slowly looked up and found his dad standing on the platform, Kenny at his side, his face all red like a tomato. Slowly he retreated behind the protection of Holly's long coat. Now he was going to get it. No video games, no television for a week, and no playing with Raymond or Kenny after school until probably forever.

"I stopped by Kenny's to pick you up, Scout," his dad said, his eyebrow arched. "I thought we'd go out and get those reindeer for the roof." He crossed his arms over his chest. "But you weren't there. Kenny's mom was about to call the police until I told her I knew where you both were.''

Eric squirmed uneasily, clutching Holly's hand so hard he might break her fingers. He knew coming here was a risk, but he had no choice. ''We were just standing near the bus stop,'' he explained. ''And then the bus came and...we just hopped on!''

''Yeah,'' Kenny said. ''We were only gonna see who was inside, but then the doors closed and off we went.''

''Off we went,'' Eric repeated. He sighed, then stepped out from behind Holly. ''All right, it wasn't really like that, but I—I don't care if you're mad. I had to get my angel back.''

The conductor picked up the step from the platform and hopped onto the car behind Holly. He blew his whistle and called out, ''All aboard.''

''Holly has to go home,'' Alex said. ''Her train is leaving.''

''No,'' Holly murmured.

His gaze snapped from Eric to her. ''What?''

They stared at each other for a long time, Eric glancing between the two, his face wrinkled into a frown. There was something funny going on here. Holly was staring at his dad the same way Eleanor Winchell stared at Raymond when she told him she loved him and wanted to marry him. And his dad was staring at Holly the same way Kenny stared at Eric's Michael Jordan rookie card.

''I don't have to go home. I'll stay until Christmas.'' She drew in a deep breath, then started toward the station, missing the stunned look on his father's face and the long breath of air that came out of him like a stuck balloon. Eric's dad started after her, leaving Kenny and Eric standing on the platform.

Kenny wiggled his eyebrows and laughed raucously. "Kissy, kissy," he murmured, puckering his lips.

Eric frowned. Could his Christmas angel be falling in love with his dad? And could his dad feel the same way about Holly? "You really think so?" he asked.

"Hey, I was the one who broke the news to Raymond about Eleanor Winchell. I know all about chicks. Your dad has the hots for your angel. And I think she feels the same way."

Eric took a moment to digest the notion, then grinned. "Cool," he raved. He grabbed Kenny's hand and ran after Holly. When he caught up to her, he took her hand and swung it between them. "When we get home, can we make that gingerbread house from the magazine? The one with the gumdrops on the top?"

"We can do whatever you want," Holly said.

"Good," Eric said with a secret smile. "'Cause my dad really loves gingerbread."

5

THE HOUSE WAS FILLED with the scent of warm spices, cloves and cinnamon and ginger. An ''Alvin and the Chipmunks'' Christmas album chirped cheerily from the stereo while Eric sat at the end of the counter squeezing icing onto freshly baked gingerbread men. His lack of coordination made the men look as if they'd just returned from a gingerbread war, eyes and mouths displaced, pants hanging down over feet, hands mangled. But Holly was beginning to realize that perfection didn't always come from appearances. Instead it came from the joy on the frosting-stained face of a little boy she was slowly growing to love.

The pieces to a gingerbread house were cooling on the table as Holly pulled a gingerbread cake from the oven, the fragrance swirling in the air in front of her. ''How's it going?'' she asked Eric. ''Are you almost finished?'' She snatched up a cookie and took a bite. ''Yummy!''

Eric put another flourish of frosting on the last man, then sat back, pensive. ''We should have some gingerbread girls,'' he finally said. ''You know, in case the boys get horny.''

Holly nearly choked on the cookie, coughing and patting her chest, her eyes watering. ''Wh-what?''

''It's not good to have all boys. It's like us, here at the farm—me, Dad and Gramps. When it's all boys it's not as much fun. We get kind of horny.''

"Hor-horny?" She schooled her voice into casual indifference. "Where did you learn this word?"

"From Raymond. He says when his dad goes away on business, he gets horny for his mom. And when he comes home, they're all happy again."

"And what do you think horny means?"

Eric rolled his eyes, as if she were the biggest idiot he'd ever met. "It's like lonely," he said, swiping a glob of frosting off the counter and popping his finger into his mouth. "It's kind of a dumb word for lonely since it reminds me of horny toads." He studied one of his gingerbread men for a long moment. "I think my dad might be horny. So it's good you're here."

Holly braced her arms on the edge of the counter and steadied herself. Without any parental experience behind her, she wasn't sure what to do. Should she gently explain the true meaning of the word to Eric? Or should she try to preserve at least a small measure of his innocence? Since she had no intention of fulfilling Alex Marrin's horny desires, she decided to let it go.

"Do you ever get horny?" Eric asked.

"No!" Holly cried, the answer coming out much louder than she intended. "No. Never."

"Hmm. I guess it must only be boys then." He twisted until he was kneeling on the kitchen stool, his elbows braced on the counter. "You should take some of that cake down to the barn for my dad," he suggested. "Since he didn't come up for dinner, he must be really hungry."

Holly considered his suggestion for a moment. Alex probably was hungry and the gingerbread could serve as a peace offering of sorts. Besides, she hated living in limbo like she was, not knowing what he was thinking or how he felt. If she were going to spend another two weeks in this house, they'd have to develop some kind of truce or Eric would begin to notice the tension between them. "You're right," she murmured. "Why don't you get back to the library and finish your homework? And when you're finished, make sure you take a bath and wash all that frosting from your hair. Your grandfather can help you. Tell him I've gone down to the barn. He's in the library watching television."

A wide grin split Eric's serious expression. "Great! And don't forget the coffee. Cream and two sugars. That's the way my dad likes it." With that, he raced off to find his grandfather, his footsteps echoing through the empty house. But a few moments later, he ran back into the kitchen, breathless, his eyes bright. "Can you take the ribbon out of your hair?"

Holly frowned, then reached back and pulled the ribbon and the elastic from her haphazard ponytail. Her hair tumbled around her face and Eric smiled and nodded. "There," he said, "that's better." A second later, he was gone again.

Holly quickly tidied up the kitchen, stacking the gingerbread men at one end of the counter. Then she sliced a generous chunk of the warm gingerbread cake, wrapped it in a clean dish towel and filled a battered thermos with coffee. She checked her reflection in the kitchen window before she tugged on her wool jacket, slipped on her boots and made her way down to the barns.

Both barns were brightly illuminated, light spilling out of the high windows to sparkle in the snow. Holly chose the north barn, yanking open the heavy door and slipping inside. She wandered down the aisle, peeking into each stall, but Alex was nowhere to be found. She turned around and—

"Hi," he murmured. He stood in the center of the aisle, his hair damp with perspiration, his shirt unbuttoned to the waist. His forearms, so well muscled, gleamed. He didn't move and seemed unable to take his eyes off of her.

She held out the thermos and the gingerbread. "I—I brought you some coffee, and a slice of gingerbread cake. Eric helped me make it."

Alex quickly removed his leather gloves, then took the proffered snack. "Thanks," he murmured, moving to take a seat on a nearby bale of straw.

Holly rubbed her hands together, glancing around nervously. "Well, I should get going, I've got—"

"Stay," he said. "You can share my snack." He slid over to make a place for her on the bale, then poured coffee into the top of the thermos and handed it to her. "I almost didn't recognize you in those clothes," he said, splitting off a piece of gingerbread cake for her. "You look like you belong here."

He should recognize the clothes, she mused, since he'd picked them all up from the snow that afternoon and returned them to her room in the tack house. Her mind wandered to an image of him folding her underwear, but she brushed it from her mind. Holly clasped her hands over her knees. "You didn't come up to the house for supper."

"I thought maybe you'd rather I stayed away."

Holly sighed. "This is your house, Alex. I'm just a guest here."

He drew a deep breath. "Then tell me," he said. "What are we supposed to do?"

She twisted her fingers together, staring at them. Better that than staring at his naked chest, contemplating the soft line of hair that started at his collarbone and ended somewhere below the button on his jeans. "I don't think it would be wrong for us to be friends," she suggested.

"I'm going to be here until Christmas. If you plan to avoid me, you're going to be spending a lot of time in this barn."

"It's not so bad out here," he said. "I've got a lot to do. And though I love my horses, I'm not tempted to kiss them." Already, she'd grown familiar with his dry wit and his self-deprecating humor. Grinning, he took the cup of coffee from her hand and took a sip, then another bite of the gingerbread. He moaned softly, then shook his head. "You're really good at this. This cake is wonderful. There is more, isn't there?"

"Up in the kitchen." Holly hid her pleasure at his compliment, searching for a change of subject so he'd stop staring at her the way he was. And so she'd resist the urge to brush her fingertips over his chest. "What do you do out here with all your time?" she asked.

"You really want to know? I didn't think you were much of a farm girl, after your first experience in the barn—your Stony Creek pedicure."

Holly felt her cheeks warm. "It's not so bad once you get used to the smell. And have a proper pair of boots. Though this place could use some potpourri and a few barrels of lemon oil, I think—"

"Potpourri?"

"It's a mix of different dried flowers, sometimes spices or herbs. You put it in sachets and you can heat it in water. It gives the room a wonderful ambience. Or you can tuck it in a lingerie drawer."

He put on a serious expression. "I've always thought my lingerie drawer needed a…what was it?"

"Sachet," Holly said, giggling. "I have a recipe for a Christmas blend with dried apples and cinnamon sticks. And another with pine needles. Although you'd probably need a truckful of the stuff to make this place smell like a lady's boudoir.''

"Yeah," Alex said. "And the effort would be lost on the horses. If it smells like apples, they'd probably eat it."

The teasing give-and-take of their conversation surprised her. She'd anticipated nothing but tension between them, but the easy set of his shoulders, his crooked smile, told her differently. Maybe they could be just friends.

"Would you like me to show you around?" Alex offered after he finished the last bite of gingerbread cake. "You didn't get much of a tour that first day."

Holly nodded. He stood and held out his hand to her, then pulled it back when he realized they probably shouldn't touch each other again. He covered his blunder by shoving his hand into his jeans pocket and taking another sip of his coffee. In truth, Holly would have liked to hold his hand, but maybe this was for the best.

Side by side, they strolled down the long aisle that ran the length of the barn. Holly peered into a stall, bracing her arms on the edge of the high gate. A pretty brown mare kept one eye on her and the other on the food she was munching. Unlike the vicious beast, Scirocco, this horse looked sweet and docile. "Who's this?"

"This is Jade. Her official name is Greenmeadow Girl. But we always give our mares nicknames. Usually precious gems or flowers."

"Eric was complaining that there were no girls on the farm. I guess he forgot about all the horses," Holly said.

A frown wrinkled Alex's perfect brow. "He was complaining?"

"Yeah." She laughed softly, then sent him a sideways glance. "And make a note to talk to him about the meaning of the word 'horny.' He has it confused with lonely."

Alex's eyes widened and he gasped. "What do you two talk about when you're baking?"

"That's strictly between us," Holly said with a sly smile. She climbed up on the first rung of the gate. "So is Jade going to have a baby?"

"A foal. And yes, she is."

"Who delivers the baby?"

"They kind of take care of that on their own. Sometimes they need my help or the vet's. Hopefully it'll happen after the first of the year."

"Why is that?" Holly asked. "For tax purposes?"

Alex chuckled. "If they're born before January 1, they're considered a two-year-old at next January's auction, instead of a yearling. So if Jade foals early, we usually don't bother discovering that foal until after the first of the year."

"This seems like a lot of work for just you and your father."

"We've got a couple of high school kids that come in every evening and on weekends to clean stalls and groom the horses. It's not hard work when you love your job."

Holly nodded. "I guess not." She moved to hop off the gate, but her heel caught and she stumbled. In an instant, Alex's hands circled her waist, steadying her as he lowered her to the ground. But this time he didn't draw away. Instead he idly smoothed his hands from her waist to her hips.

It was Holly who broke the spell, Holly who took a step back. She forced a smile. "I'd better finish cleaning up the kitchen. I'll leave the gingerbread cake out for you."

He nodded, the barest hint of gratitude curling his lips. "I suppose I'll see you tomorrow?"

"Tomorrow," Holly murmured. Her pulse pounding,

she spun on her heel and hurried out of the barn. But she didn't slow her pace until she reached the house. She stopped, her hand on the door, her quickened breath clouding in the cold air.

She could still feel the warm imprint of his hands on her waist and she groaned softly. "If this is what gingerbread and coffee does to the man, I better not try my lemon meringue pie on him."

ALEX STOMPED THE SNOW OFF his boots, then pushed open the back door to the house. He'd been working in the barn all day, taking a short break only for the sandwiches Jed brought down at noon. But he'd finished all his work in anticipation of a Christmas tradition that hadn't been observed since before Renee left.

It was one of his favorite holiday activities, a tradition that he remembered from his own childhood. He and Jed had tossed the tarp off the old cutter and wiped down the cracked leather seats. He'd gathered up a stack of clean blankets, oiled the jingle-bell traces and given Daisy a grooming until her winter coat shone.

As he stepped inside, he drew a deep breath, new and tempting odors assailing him every time he returned to the house. He'd become continually amazed at the transformation Holly had wrought. Room by room, his house was becoming a Christmas showcase, filled with beautiful decorations, fragrant garlands, twinkling lights and candles. And still, the florist trucks arrived with more, the deliveryman from Dalton's hauling yet another bag of decorations up the front steps, and Jed, as besotted by Holly as Eric, squired her around town to every shop that carried Christmas merchandise.

He found Holly in her usual spot, in front of the stove, peering into a steaming pot of water. "What are you cooking up now?'' he asked, stepping to the sink to wash his hands. He grabbed a towel from the rack, then noticed it had pretty little embroidered Christmas trees along the hem. He carefully replaced it, then wiped his damp hands on the thighs of his jeans.

"It's wonderful! Perfect!" Holly murmured. "Look, I found a mold in the back of the cupboard."

"There's mold in the—"

"No, a mold. It must be at least a hundred years old. Collectors pay exorbitant amounts for these things. I probably shouldn't even be using it but—"

"There's stuff in this house that my great-grandmother cooked with," Alex said. "You should see the attic. So what's so special about this?"

"I think it's an English mold, made especially for plum pudding. That's what I'm making. It's steaming in the pot right now. We'll have it with Christmas dinner."

"Hmm," Alex said. "I like pudding. But where did you get the plums?"

Holly glanced over at him with an odd expression, as if she'd just realized he was there. Sometimes she got so wrapped up in her Christmas preparations she lost all contact with reality. "There are no plums in plum pudding. It's a traditional Christmas dessert made with raisins and figs and suet and bread."

Alex wrinkled his nose. "Suet?"

"Yes. It steams for six hours and then you wrap it in a brandy-soaked cloth until Christmas. And then you re-warm it and drizzle hard sauce over it."

Wasn't suet what Jed fed the chickadees? So far, he'd loved everything Holly had offered him, but suet? "Hard sauce. And that's made with...let me guess...nuts and bolts? Or maybe gravel?"

Holly rolled her eyes. "I guarantee you're going to love

it. I haven't made a plum pudding since I was very young. We always used to have it at my house for Christmas dinner.''

He nodded, then moved to the cookie jar to see what new treat awaited him today. ''Then you're going to stay for Christmas dinner?'' he asked, trying to sound nonchalant.

Holly shifted uneasily. ''My contract requires that I stay, unless you don't want me to stay. It's entirely up to you.''

''No, no,'' Alex said. ''I wouldn't want you to be in breach of your contract.'' They stood in uncomfortable silence for a long moment. ''So, are you almost ready to go?'' he asked. ''Make sure you dress warm. Once the sun goes down, it gets chilly.''

''Where are we going?''

''Didn't Eric tell you? I'm taking you both out for a sleigh ride as soon as he gets home from school. I've got Daisy all hitched up. It's a full moon tonight, so we'll be able to see.''

''Oh, that sounds like fun!'' Holly cried. The color rose in her cheeks with barely suppressed excitement. Alex felt a flood of warmth race through his body at her natural beauty. She was dressed much like she had been last night in the barn, in casual clothes, her wavy flaxen hair pinned up in a careless knot with tendrils brushing her face.

Right on cue, Alex heard the front door slam and Eric came stomping through the house, dragging his backpack behind him. ''Hey, Scout!''

''Hey, Dad. Hey, Holly.''

''Why don't you change real quick and put on a warmer jacket. Remember, we're going to take Holly out in the sleigh.''

Eric glanced between Holly and Alex, then hesitantly

shook his head. "I—I can't, Dad. I know I promised this morning, but Kenny has this science project he has to do and he needs my help. His mom is coming right over to pick me up and I'm supposed to have supper with them. It's really important."

Alex studied his son shrewdly. Somehow, he didn't think Eric was being entirely truthful. He had that same tight smile he used when he was faking sick before school or covering up a bad report from his teacher. "But I have this all planned. Are you sure you don't want to go?"

"It's not that I don't want to go. I can't." Eric swallowed and pasted an even tighter grin on his face. "It's ignorant rocks. Kenny doesn't know anything about them and I have to help him."

"Ignorant rocks? Don't you mean igneous?"

"Yeah, that's it. So why don't you and Holly go anyway? I wouldn't want her to miss it." He turned to Holly. "It's the most fun."

Alex nodded, suddenly aware of his son's motivations. His heart twisted in his chest and he cursed silently. He should have been prepared for this. There was no way Eric could avoid seeing Holly as a potential mate for his dad. She was pretty and smart and exactly the kind of woman a boy like Eric might wish for his new mother. But building up his hopes, only to have them dashed when Holly left, was something that Alex could not allow. It had taken Eric almost a year to get over his mother's desertion. How long would he mourn after Holly left?

"All right," Alex said. "We'll just cancel for today. We can go another day."

"No!" Eric cried. "I—I mean, today is the best day. And—and what if the snow melts? Then Holly wouldn't get a sleigh ride at all."

A car horn beeped outside the front door and Eric

snatched up his backpack and ran out of the room. "I gotta go!"

"Have Kenny's mom bring you home by eight," Alex called.

"Bye, Dad. Bye, Holly. Have fun!"

The door slammed behind him and Alex leaned back against the counter, crossing his arms over his chest. "I guess it's just the two of us. Unless you don't want to go," he murmured.

"No, I'd like to go. As long as you have Daisy all hitched up. And the moon is full. Besides, I already finished my report on ignorant rocks."

Alex laughed. "Then grab your mittens and hat and let's go."

"Wait," Holly said. "I'll make some hot chocolate and wrap up some cookies."

"You do that and meet me at the barn," he said. He pulled his gloves from his pockets, then strode to the back door. "Don't be too long." But she didn't hear him. She was already dumping milk into a pan and dropping in a chunk of chocolate, lost again in plans, this time for a perfect sleigh ride.

Alex ambled down to the barn, whistling a cheery version of "Jingle Bells" as he walked. He found Daisy waiting in front of the north barn, Jed adjusting her harnesses.

"Where're Holly and the boy?" he asked.

"Eric has a school project he's doing with Kenny. Holly is whipping up some hot chocolate. She'll be along in a few minutes."

Jed raised his eyebrow. "Eric's not going along?"

"Naw," Alex replied. He noticed the leery look on his father's face. "Do you want to come and be our chaperone?"

Jed laughed, then rubbed his stubbled chin. "You want me to come along? If you're scared to be alone with the little lady, I can always—"

"I'm not afraid to be with her," he protested. "We're getting along just fine now that we've come to an agreement."

"What's that? An agreement to pretend that you don't care about her? Well, that's the dumbest thing I ever did hear."

"That's the way she wants it," Alex said.

"What a woman says she wants and what she really wants are sometimes very different. Haven't you figured that out yet?"

"All I know is that I'm not going to be kissing her again, that's for sure—unless she asks. And I don't expect that anytime soon."

His father chuckled and shook his head. "Holing yourself up at this farm for the past two years hasn't done you any good, son. If you really want that little lady, then let her know. Sooner or later, she'll come over to your way of thinking."

"And what is my way of thinking?" Alex asked.

"Why, I suspect, you're in love with her. You just haven't realized it yet." He gave Daisy a pat on the neck, then wandered back toward the barn, mumbling to himself.

"I barely know her!" Alex called.

Jed turned around. "That's right. We Marrin men don't need much time. It was that way with your grandpa and your great-grandpa and me. When we see the gal we want, we get matters settled right off."

"But I only knew Renee for three months before I decided to marry her. And that didn't work out."

Jed nodded. "Yep. I coulda predicted that. You took

too long in deciding. Three months. That one was doomed from the start.''

Alex muttered a soft oath as his father walked into the barn, then efficiently began to rearrange the blankets beneath the seats. Jed had refilled the kerosene lamps that decorated the front corners of the cutter and even tossed in an old moth-eaten lap robe that he remembered from his childhood rides.

Though he tried to occupy himself with preparations for their ride, he couldn't ignore his father's words. Was he really falling in love with Holly Bennett? How could that be? He'd known her less than a week. He couldn't possibly fall in love in a week!

Alex stepped back from the cutter and raked his hands through his hair. Alone with Holly, snuggled beneath cozy blankets, in the midst of a moonlit night. This was an evening planned for lovers.

''Maybe this wasn't such a good idea after all,'' he muttered.

HOLLY'S SPIRITS SOARED as they skimmed over the snow. The jingle bells on the horse's reins rang sharp and clear in the silence of the outdoors. The only other sounds, the creak of old leather and the dull thud of the horse's hooves in the snow, played a strangely soothing counterpoint in the waning light of day.

Here in the crisp evening air, she felt the spirit of the season surround her, engulf her, until she had no choice but to laugh out loud. They glided through rolling snow-covered meadows, pastures for the horses in the summer, down lanes flanked by old stone fences that divided forest from field, and through lightly wooded glades, where the bare trees shivered in the wind.

Her cheeks and nose, ruddy with the cold, were nearly

numb, but the rest of her body was toasty warm beneath the heavy lap robe. Alex urged Daisy into a quick trot and they flew through a drift of snow, the sleigh rising up in the air. Holly screamed before she hit the seat with a bump, then giggled.

"Whoa! Slow down there, Daisy," Alex called. They rounded a short bend in the lane and then he drew the horse to a stop. Holly looked out on the vista, a wide expanse of land that dropped gently to a winding creek below. The shallow water, not yet frozen, bubbled over rocks and glinted in the low angle of the setting sun. "That's Stony Creek," he said.

The sun hung low over the horizon, streaking the sky with pink and gold. "I don't think I've ever seen a more beautiful spot," Holly murmured. "Your farm seems to be blessed with so many pretty spots."

Alex smiled. "I think so, too. And every season brings something new. There's a grove of wild plum trees just down there that burst into bloom in the spring. As a kid, I used to ride out here in the fall and pick the plums from the back of my horse. My mom would turn them into jam."

"Does Eric do that now?"

Alex shook his head. "Naw. No one to turn the plums into jam."

Holly sighed. "Maybe I'll come back in the fall and do that for him. I've never made wild plum jam. I'll bet it's good."

"You'd do that?" Alex asked, his gaze intense, skimming the features of her face as if he were trying to read her mind, discern her true intentions.

"Of course. Why not?" she said, covering her offer with an air of indifference.

"I just figured you'd go back to the city and forget all about us," Alex said.

Holly felt the heat rise in her cheeks, driving away the cold. She tore her gaze from his and stared out at the landscape. "I don't think I could ever forget this place. It's given me back Christmas." She distracted herself by tucking the robe around her legs. "These past few years, I've almost dreaded the holidays. It's all been about business. I work and work to make everyone else's Christmas perfect and when Christmas Eve finally comes, I'm left wondering why I feel so sad."

"We're two of a kind, then," Alex said. "I always tried to work up some enthusiasm for Eric's sake, but the holidays just brought back bad memories."

"But this Christmas is different for me," Holly continued. "I'm happy. Joyous might be a better word." She turned to face him, only to find his eyes already fixed on her.

Slowly he reached over and brushed a strand of wind-whipped hair from her cheek, then hesitantly drew his hand away. "I'm happy, too," he murmured. The deeper meaning of his words hung between them in the cold air and Holly didn't need to question the cause of Alex's happiness. It was there in his expression, the smile that barely touched his lips, the warm light in his eyes. She swallowed hard, willing him to lean closer and kiss her, for this time, she wouldn't fight him. This time she wanted him.

But when he refused to make a move, Holly nearly screamed in frustration. What was stopping him? She certainly acted like she wanted him to kiss her, didn't she? Short of closing her eyes, throwing herself at his chest and puckering up, how much more obvious could she be?

But as moments passed, excruciatingly long moments, she remembered his words after the last time they kissed.

She groaned inwardly. Did he really expect her to beg? Oh, this was just like him, to taunt her with her own reservations, to make her feel all warm and mushy inside, then coldly refuse to respond. Well, she could be just as hard-hearted as he was. She didn't need his kisses and she'd prove it!

Holly sat back in the seat. "Let's go," she said.

He arched his eyebrow, his smile turning sardonic. "Do you want to drive?"

Holly took the reins from his hands. If he wanted her in control, then she'd take control! "All right. This doesn't look too hard. There's no clutch, no gearbox. What do I do?"

He wrapped an arm around her shoulder and took her hands in his. "Weave the reins through your fingers like this. Give it a firm touch, but not too firm. She needs to know you're in control." He raised Holly's hands and let the reins drop gently against Daisy's rump. "Hup, Daisy girl. Get along."

The horse lurched into action, quickly breaking into a brisk trot. Holly clutched the reins and fixed her eyes on the horse's bobbing head. But her mind was focused on the feel of Alex's arm around her shoulders, the warmth that seeped through his jacket, the faint scent of his aftershave. She'd never known a man to smell as…manly as Alex Marrin. No fancy designer cologne nor expensive shampoo, just all man—rugged, windblown, suntanned man.

The further they went, the more her mind wandered, to thoughts of his smooth, muscled chest, his flat belly, the sinewy strength of his arms. Shoulders so broad and a waist so narrow it made her ache with the need to look at him. Piece by piece, she mentally removed his clothes until—

Holly coughed softly. "How do I stop?" she demanded, her voice cracking slightly.

Alex looked down at her, his chin grazing her temple. "Stop?"

"Yes!" she cried. "How do I stop the horse? I want to stop now."

"Pull back," he said. "Whoa, Daisy. Whoa, girl."

When the cutter slid to a stop, she shoved the reins back into his hands. He swung his arm over her head, a perplexed expression on his face. "Do you want to go back to the house?" he asked.

Holly shook her head. "No."

"What do you want?"

"I—I want you to kiss me," she said. She drew in a deep breath, then let it out very slowly, clouding the air in front of her face. Until now, she'd listened to her head instead of her heart. But suddenly her head was starting to agree with her heart.

Why shouldn't she have exactly what she wanted? She'd spent her whole career planning for the future, waiting for Christmas to come. It was about time she lived for now, lived for this very moment when desire danced between them. "I'm not going to ask again," Holly murmured. "I'm not going to beg. So, if you want to kiss me, you'd better do it now or lose your chance."

He chuckled softly. "You think I want to kiss you?"

Her head snapped around and she narrowed her eyes. "Don't you?"

Alex shrugged lazily. "I'm not sure. I hadn't really thought about it."

An aggravated moan slipped from her throat and she pushed aside the lap robe and slid to the far edge of the seat. All she wanted was a simple kiss. Why did he have to make it so difficult? "Then don't. I don't care. I—I just thought you might want to. You looked like you did."

"Maybe I do," Alex finally said, a wicked grin twitching at his lips. "But with you over there and me over here. Well…" He lifted the lap robe, inviting her back beneath its warmth. When she relented and slid over the cracked leather seat, he slipped his arm back around her shoulders and she grudgingly settled against him. But he still didn't make a move.

"You can do it anytime now," she muttered.

He caught her chin with his finger and turned her face up until she was forced to look at him. "The truth is, I want to kiss you," he said, bending nearer, "wherever and whenever I want. I want to be able to pull you into my arms and taste your mouth. And I want you to kiss me back, to go soft against me, to wrap your arms around my neck and run your fingers through my hair."

"I—I can do that," Holly stammered, staring into his eyes, aware of the passion burning there. All her resolve vanished and Holly was certain of what she wanted. "Really, I can."

"Then maybe we should give it a try?"

Dazed, she blinked and waited, waited for that exquisite moment when his lips would touch hers, that instant when his tongue would take possession of her mouth. And then it happened, a kiss she'd been waiting for her entire adult life, from a man she'd been searching for since she'd first become aware of the opposite sex. And it all happened as he said it would, lips touching, tongues tasting, and her heart threatening to burst from her chest.

She slipped her arms around his neck and furrowed her fingers through his hair. A soft moan rumbled deep in his throat and the kiss gradually intensified, growing more frantic with every passing breath. He took her face between his hands and molded her mouth to his, stealing her breath and making her pulse race even faster.

Holly felt giddy, light-headed, so much so that she forgot to think and merely felt. All her doubts and insecurities vanished as desire surged between them and a simple kiss became so much more. She brushed aside his canvas jacket and pressed her palms against his warm chest, the flannel of his shirt soft beneath her fingertips.

But that wasn't enough for Holly. She wanted to touch him, really touch him, to feel his skin beneath her hands. With shaking fingers, she unbuttoned his shirt, craving his warmth. He did the same, unzipping her jacket and slipping his hands beneath her sweater to circle her waist. On and on, the kiss went, never breaking contact, growing more desperate until they nearly tore at each other's clothes.

Holly had almost dispensed with the buttons of his shirt when she was thwarted by yet another layer, his thermal undershirt. His lips still clinging to hers, Alex yanked both shirts out of the waistband of his jeans. He grabbed her hands and slid them beneath, her fingers skimming over the rippled muscles of his stomach until she felt his heart beating beneath her palms.

Alex slowly leaned her back onto the cool leather of the seat, drawing the lap robe around them and shutting out the cold night air. As he nuzzled Holly's neck, she opened her eyes to see a single star gleaming in the deep blue sky. She smiled and tried to think of a wish, then closed her eyes again when she realized she wanted nothing more than what she had at this very moment.

As he trailed kisses along her neck, Holly arched beneath him. Perhaps she did want more. Naked limbs twined beneath twisted sheets. The sweet weight of Alex Marrin stretched over her body. Desire so intense that nothing could satisfy it but the ultimate act of passion. Though that wouldn't happen tonight, Holly knew it would happen soon.

Now that they'd taken the first step, there would be nothing to do but rush headlong toward the inevitable, a runaway horse headed straight for the edge of a cliff. But Holly wasn't afraid. Even if they parted ways on Christmas Day, she'd always have her one perfect Christmas with Alex Marrin, a Christmas filled with passion and excitement. And those memories would be enough to last all the Christmases of her life.

She tugged his head back, then gently kissed him, running her tongue along the crease of his mouth before drawing away. "I packed some hot chocolate and cookies. Maybe we should take a break."

He smiled languidly then braced his hands on either side of her head. He wouldn't push her. Holly saw it in the way he looked at her. Alex was willing to wait until she was ready and that made her want him even more. He gave her a quick kiss, rubbed his nose against hers and sat up. "I've learned one thing from you, Holly Bennett."

She sat up beside him, straightening her clothes. "And what's that?"

"When you offer me food, I'd be a fool to refuse."

Holly tipped her head back and laughed. Alex wrapped his arms around her and hugged her tight, then nuzzled the top of her head. "And when I offer you kisses?" she asked.

''Well, given the choice, I think I'd give up the cookies, and the cake, and anything else you'd offer. The way to a man's heart is not always through his stomach.''

6

―――――

"A LITTLE TO THE LEFT… No, now a little bit back toward the right. Okay, up, up, up. Oh, there. Stop. Don't move."

Alex balanced on the ladder, his arm outstretched, his hand clutching the fresh pine garland that Holly had purchased for the front porch. He'd already affixed a lush swag of fruits and nuts and greenery just above the front door and hung tiny wreaths in all the windows on the facade of the house, but the garland seemed to be taking an inordinate amount of effort. He'd already sneezed five times and he could feel another tickle growing in his nose from the scent of evergreen.

He rubbed his nose, which threw off his balance, which set the ladder to wobbling. Alex had no choice but to drop the garland and grab hold with both hands, or take a nasty tumble into the bushes.

"Oh, no!" Holly cried. "That won't do."

Alex stared down at the garland, now draped over the yews that fronted the porch. "I think it looks nice right where it is," he said. "Besides, my arms are getting sore. Can't we just tack it up and be done with it?"

Holly shook her head and grabbed the garland, handing it back up to him. "It has to hang evenly or you'll notice it every time you drive in the driveway. It has to be—"

"Perfect," Alex completed. "Yeah, I kind of figured that."

She hitched her hands on her waist and giggled. "I'll

make you a deal. If you help me finish this, I'll be very, very grateful after you crawl down from that ladder.''

''And will that gratitude be expressed in the form of a kiss?'' he asked, holding the garland back up on the eave of the porch.

''You'll just have to wait and see.''

The past three days had been near perfect. Holly had busied herself with decorating the house and baking Christmas treats. She'd crafted delicate snowflakes from frosting and made a wreath out of tiny shiny ornaments. She'd filled the house with candles and, in the evening, lit them all, suffusing the house with wonderful scents. And after the day's work was finished and Eric had been tucked into bed, he and Holly would curl up on the sofa, the fire crackling and the tree twinkling, and talk as if they'd known each other for years.

Though he wasn't really sure what had brought about the change in her, he wasn't about to question it. He felt like a teenager again, stealing kisses while the late movie played, wondering just how far he could go before she said no. It had been so hard to hold back, for he wanted nothing more than to possess Holly, both body and soul. But after their shaky start, he wasn't willing to risk another retreat. If she ran again, he wouldn't have the courage to bring her back. A desertion now would likely tear him apart.

''That's it!'' Holly cried. ''Hold it right there.'' She scurried to collect the hammer and nails they were using to fix the garland to the porch, then handed them up to him.

When the garland was finally perfect, Alex stepped down from the ladder. He tossed the hammer into the snow, snaked his arm around Holly's waist and yanked her against him. ''Now, for that kiss.''

He dipped her back and kissed her thoroughly, making her sigh with need. And when he'd had enough, he didn't stop, but delved into her mouth just once more in case he didn't have another chance to sneak a kiss until that evening.

A low rumble sounded from the end of the driveway and Alex groaned as the school bus rolled to a stop on the road. He set Holly upright, straightened her jacket, then grinned. "Eric's home."

She gave his hand a squeeze, holding it behind her back until they saw Eric through the trees. They hadn't really discussed their relationship. Though Alex was certain it was a relationship, talking about it might make it seem too real, too fragile and too temporary. But one thing was understood—they'd keep their attraction a secret from Eric. It was for the best because Alex knew his son harbored some hope that Holly would become a permanent part of their lives.

But Alex also knew Holly had a life back in New York City, full of parties and theater and sophisticated friends— and a fiancé she'd neglected to mention in days. He'd love to believe she'd stay, but giving up a career and her plans for the future for life on an upstate horse farm, becoming an instant mother to a seven-year-old boy, wasn't something most women would choose to take on. He had to be satisfied with the time they had together. When her job was finished, he'd let her go.

"Dad!" Eric called, waving as he ran up the driveway. "I have to talk to you." He raced up to the porch and threw his backpack on the steps. "In private."

"Am I going to be making a call to Miss Green?"

"No! It's something else." He glanced at Holly. "Man talk."

Holly grabbed up the tools they'd used. "I've got some

decorating to finish inside. We'll have supper around five if that's all right.''

"Six," Eric said. "Me and my dad have stuff to do."

Alex smiled at Holly and she returned the favor, sending a flood of warmth through his bloodstream. Every day, she was more beautiful. He wondered what stroke of luck had sent this angel knocking at his door. Who was responsible? If he ever found out, he'd have to make a point to thank the person.

When Holly had closed the door behind her, Alex sat down on the porch step and patted the spot beside him. But Eric refused the invitation. "We have to go right now."

"Where?" Alex asked.

"Shopping. We have to get Christmas presents for Holly. She's going to be here on Christmas morning and she has to have something to open." He grabbed Alex's hand and pulled him to his feet. "If we go now, we can be back before dinnertime. And she won't even know."

Alex hadn't thought about a gift for Holly. Knowing her, she'd pick out the perfect present for the two of them, a thoughtful gift filled with obvious meaning. But what was he supposed to choose for a woman who wasn't his girlfriend or his lover, a woman who had wandered into his life and would soon wander out? It would take time to find the perfect gift for Holly, one that would say just enough about his feelings but not too much.

"Then we better get going," Alex said, jogging toward the pickup parked in the driveway.

"We only have eight shopping days until Christmas," Eric reminded him.

Alex pulled open the truck door and jumped inside, then reached over to open Eric's door. When his son had his seat belt fastened, he started the truck and steered it down the driveway and onto the road into town.

Eric wriggled in his seat, zipping and unzipping his jacket. "I have to get just the most perfect present."

"I'm sure anything you get Holly will be fine," Alex murmured, his mind on his own choices. Perfume? Candy? A pretty sweater?

"No, it has to be special. If I get her the right present, then maybe she'll stay."

Alex was tempted to stop the truck in the middle of the road and set his son straight. But he couldn't deny that he harbored some of the same hopes. Was there a chance she'd stay? If he said the right thing, did the right thing, would she consider giving up her life in New York? "Scout, I don't think that's the right reason to get Holly a gift. You should get her something because she's been nice to us and because she made your Christmas wish come true. But you can't expect her to give up her life and her job to stay with us."

Eric shrugged. "It could happen."

They drove for a long time in silence, Alex's eyes fixed on the road, but his thoughts elsewhere. He'd always anticipated problems with Eric when it came to a new woman in their lives. Eric still held Renee up as the ultimate mom, even though she only saw him a few times each year. They had a special connection that couldn't be diminished by time apart.

"Would you like to have a new mom?" Alex asked.

"I know my mom isn't coming back to live with us. And I think you need a wife."

"Don't worry about me," Alex said. "I'm doing all right."

A light snow started to fall as they reached the downtown area. Alex found a parking space just off the square and he and Eric joined the holiday shoppers as they hurried toward Dalton's. Eric didn't even bother to linger over the windows, so intent was he on his mission.

They passed through the revolving doors and stopped once inside. "So what were you thinking about?" Alex asked, hoping his son might be able to give him a few pointers. He'd never been much good at figuring out what women liked. And Holly would be very particular about the perfume she wore or the scarves she chose.

Eric grabbed his hand and dragged him over to the far side of the main floor, past perfume, past accessories and directly to jewelry. He pressed his nose up against the glass case and carefully scrutinized a selection of precious gemstones fashioned into earrings, rings and necklaces. "These are pretty," he said.

"And a little out of your price range," Alex said.

"How much?" Eric asked the salesperson.

The man perused the case. "The least expensive item would be the birthstone earrings. They're ninety-nine."

Eric glanced up at his father. "I have ninety-nine cents," he said.

Alex smiled and placed his hand on Eric's head. "I think he means dollars."

A crestfallen expression suffused Eric's face. But then he suddenly brightened. "You could buy her the earrings. Or a bracelet. Or a diamond ring." He looked up at the salesman. "Do you have any diamond rings?"

The salesman gave Alex a questioning look, then proceeded to the next case. "We have some lovely rings here. Do you know what style she likes? We have brilliant cut, marquis, emerald cut, and a variety of settings in gold and platinum."

"Let's look at them all," Eric said.

Alex wasn't about to argue. In truth, he was curious.

When he married Renee, he only had enough money to buy her a cheap ring with a barely visible diamond. He wasn't even sure what an engagement ring cost. It couldn't hurt to look.

The salesman set the velvet case in front of them. Eric peered at the selections. "I think she'd like that one," he said, reaching up and pointing to the largest diamond in the front row.

"How much is that one?" Alex asked.

"This is a one-carat emerald-cut diamond of impeccable color and clarity in a platinum setting. It's just under nine thousand."

Alex blinked. "Nine thousand. That's a lot of molasses and oats."

"Excuse me?"

"Nothing." He bent down until he was eye-level with Eric. "Scout, I think we can find something else for Holly besides a diamond ring. Maybe a pretty bracelet or a sweater."

Eric gave one last look to the diamond rings then nodded. "We could sniffle some perfume," he said. "Holly always smells really good. I bet she uses a lot of that stuff."

The salesman put the diamond rings back in the case, locked it, then leaned over the counter. He motioned to Eric and the little boy pushed up on his tiptoes. "Try bath salts or scented lotion. That's what I usually get my wife for a Christmas gift and she loves it."

"I bet they have some nice gift boxes at the perfume counter," Alex suggested to his son.

Eric took one last look at the rings, then nodded. "That would probably be better. Those rings are real little. She could lose it."

Alex breathed a small sigh of relief as they strolled

back to the perfume counter. But his mind was still on the diamond rings. Which one would she like? Holly had very sophisticated taste and, though she dressed in a simple, elegant manner, she seemed to be drawn more toward traditional things. There was a pretty ring in the top row Alex was certain she'd—

He cursed to himself. What the hell was he thinking? They'd barely shared their first kiss a few days ago and he was already thinking engagement rings?

Alex sighed. If he knew what was good for him he'd head right to the scarf department.

HOLLY GLANCED AT THE CLOCK over the kitchen sink then wiped her hands on a dish towel. She'd just finished a duo of tiny pinecone wreaths that she planned to hang on either side of the library fireplace. Eric was stretched out on the sofa watching a favorite *Star Wars* video. And Alex had ventured out to the barn nearly three hours before, promising to be back in a few minutes.

She wandered over to the sofa and ruffled Eric's hair. ''Come on, buddy. It's half past nine. Time for bed.''

Except for the obligatory groan, Eric didn't protest. Pleased with another successful foray into parenting, Holly slipped him a cookie as they walked through the kitchen, then accepted his quick peck on the cheek before he crawled up the stairs. She'd never spent much time around kids and had always doubted her ability to parent. But with Eric, she'd seemed to fall into it naturally.

They were friends, but she'd also managed to cultivate a level of respect between them. Eric listened to her and did his best to please. And the rare times that he misbehaved in her presence, she'd merely have to look at him sternly and he'd shape up. But there was something more she'd found with Eric. Holly had no doubt that he cared about her, maybe even loved her. And her feelings had grown just as strong.

Now, when she thought about the day she'd leave Stony Creek Farm, she didn't only think about leaving Alex. She thought about saying goodbye to Eric. She couldn't imagine walking away from him without tears in her eyes.

Holly brushed the thoughts aside, determined not to dwell on the future. She glanced around the room. Jed had gone to bed an hour before, and with nothing else to do in the house, Holly decided to return to the tack house—after she made a quick stop in the barn. She tucked a few cookies in a cheerful linen Christmas napkin, then poured some spiced cider into Alex's thermos, before heading out.

She expected to find him hard at work or deeply involved in some project. But when she slipped through the door of the north barn, she found Alex halfway down the main aisle, his arms braced across the top rung of a stall door, his attention focused on the horse inside.

She slowly approached. "Alex, is everything all right? I thought you were coming back to the house." In truth, she'd looked forward to their time alone together all day, although she couldn't admit that aloud. Holly still wasn't sure what they were doing since neither one had broached the subject of their relationship. But without a few moments alone with him, Holly knew she'd pass a restless night, wondering if she'd done something wrong.

At the sound of her voice, Alex glanced her way, then turned back to the stall. "I don't know. She's acting restless."

Holly followed his gaze. It was Jade, the sweet-tempered mare she'd come to trust. The one she'd been sneaking sugar cubes to the past three days. "Is that bad?"

"It could mean she's going to foal early."

Holly groaned inwardly. "Or could it mean she's had too much sugar?" He frowned at her. "I'm sorry. I know I should have asked, but I've been giving her sugar every time I come down to the barn. She's the only horse who's been nice to me and I figured since we were becoming friends, I would—"

Alex pressed a finger to Holly's lips. "A few sugar cubes a day won't hurt her."

"How about six?" Holly asked, wincing.

He shook his head, then turned away. "I don't think that's the problem."

Holly sighed in relief. Good Lord, the last thing she wanted to do was kill one of Alex's horses. "Then what is?"

"She's due to foal in mid-January but last year she foaled in late November and lost the foal." He shook his head. "She's got a great pedigree. If she'd go full-term, the foal could grow to be a great horse."

"Isn't there something you can do?" Holly asked. "Couldn't you call the vet? Give her some drugs? Get her off her feet?"

"With horses, it's sometimes best to let nature take its course. Just watch and wait."

Holly sighed. He seemed so distant, so preoccupied. He'd always been attentive to her, but then they'd only been romantically involved for a few days. There were so many things she didn't know about him. Did he need her here for support or would he rather be alone? Holly wasn't sure what she was expected to do.

"I—I'll leave you to it then," she finally said. "Eric went to bed. There's some pecan pie on the stove if you're hungry and I brought you some cookies and cider." She set the thermos and the cookies on a nearby barrel. "I'm going to bed."

"Thanks," he murmured distractedly.

"All right, then. Good night."

She turned to leave, but at the last moment he caught her around the waist and pulled her close. "I'm sorry," he said, nuzzling his face in her hair. "Stay. I don't want you to leave just yet."

"But you're busy. I don't want to—"

"Looking at you always takes my mind off my problems." He turned her to face him and wrapped his arms around her waist, pressing his hips to hers.

"So, would you like to roll around in the hay?" he teased.

"Why don't we start with a kiss in the barn," she murmured, "and see where that leads."

He tipped her chin up and grazed her lips with his. Holly's knees grew weak and she wondered whether she would ever refuse him anything. With every day that passed, she needed him more—and not just in the physical sense. In the course of a single day, she'd think of so many things she wanted to tell him, little thoughts that came to her mind, bits of information she knew he'd enjoy.

A few days ago, after he'd first kissed her on their sleigh ride, she'd convinced herself that she could still walk away, that on the evening of Christmas Day, she'd pack her bags and take the train home with no regrets. All she needed to do was maintain her distance, protect her heart.

But now, she knew that was impossible. And that knowledge wouldn't change the reality of their situation. After she left, they'd never see each other again.

Holly wrapped her arms around his neck and kissed

him hard, trying to commit the kiss to memory, to burn the wonderful sensations into her brain. Someday, she'd want to remember, wouldn't she? Or would she pray to banish the memory from her mind? It really didn't matter because nothing would make her forget Alex Marrin—not time, not distance and never another man.

He responded to her passion immediately, his hands skimming over her body as his tongue plundered her mouth. Frantic with need, he scooped her up into his arms and carried her to the end of the aisle, to a huge pile of straw.

"It doesn't look very comfortable," she said.

"It's scratchy and dusty and it will get in your hair," he said.

"But every girl has to have at least one roll in the hay with a man, doesn't she?"

With a playful growl, he tossed her into the straw and she pulled him down on top of her. Dust clouded up around them and Holly sat up, sneezed once, then twice. "It always seems so romantic in the movies."

"It can be very romantic," Alex said, nibbling on her neck. "Let me show you." His hands slid beneath her jacket and he pushed it off her shoulders and tossed it aside. His fingers found the hem of her sweater, bunching it in his fist then tugging it over her head. In short order, he yanked his own flannel shirt over his head, adding it to the growing pile of clothing beside him.

Holly closed her eyes and reveled in his touch, the deft workings of his fingers as he unbuttoned her shirt. They'd never gone this far before, never ventured into such intimate territory. His lips trailed over her collarbone, then drifted lower still.

Holly's mind raced. Was this what she really wanted? Would she be able to live with herself in the morning?

And why hadn't she made these decisions earlier, before she became entangled in the heat of the moment? Her breath caught in her throat as he placed a kiss on the warm swell of her breast. And then, all the questions didn't matter. He captured her nipple, his lips damp through the sheer fabric of her bra.

She arched beneath him, moaning softly with his brazen caress, then skimmed her hands over his shoulders, his chest, his belly, conscious of every muscle, every inch of warm, hard flesh. Vague dreams that had disturbed her sleep now became reality, an intense, stirring reality that was hard to deny. She needed Alex, his touch, his taste. And his heart.

"I guess this *can* be romantic," she murmured in his ear.

Alex drew back and looked down into her eyes. "This is where I kissed my first girl."

"On this very hay?" she asked skeptically.

"No, that hay became compost a long time ago. But in this barn. In one of those stalls near the end. Her name was…" He frowned. "I can't remember her name."

"And will you remember my name?" Holly asked, reaching up to stroke his cheek.

The smile slowly faded from his face and she felt him stiffen. He opened his mouth to say something, then snapped it shut.

"Did I say something wrong?" she asked, trying to read his emotions in his eyes.

Alex shook his head and rolled off her. As an afterthought, he plucked at the front of her blouse, carefully covering exposed skin. Then he sat up, leaving her a view of the tensed muscles in his neck and back. "About that…" he said.

"What?"

"You know. When you leave. We haven't talked about it. In truth, I think we've been avoiding it."

Holly reached out to touch him and he jumped slightly. "I don't need any promises," she said. "Promises you can't keep."

"I'm just not very good at happily ever after," he said. "I don't know how to make it happen. And if we had…a future, I know that sooner or later, I'd mess up and you'd leave." He furrowed his fingers through his hair. "Maybe this was a mistake. We shouldn't form any attachments. It will only make things more difficult."

Holly quickly buttoned her blouse and reached behind him to grab her sweater. Suddenly a simple roll in the hay had turned complicated. "I—I really should go to bed. I'll see you in the morning."

She scrambled up from the pile of straw, frantically brushing the remnants from her clothes as if that might brush away the embarrassment. Why couldn't she have left well enough alone? She knew better than to bring up the future.

When she finally reached her room in the tack house, she locked herself in her bedroom and prayed that he wouldn't follow her. Right now, she needed to put Alex Marrin and all the feelings he stirred inside of her firmly aside. She had a week to go until Christmas, a week to repair the mistakes she'd made.

But try as she might, Holly couldn't regret the question she'd asked. Would he remember her after she was gone? Or would she fade into the past, a brief interlude during a magical holiday season, a fantasy that, with time, became less real?

"I'll just focus on the job," she murmured. Holly pressed her palms to her eyes and flopped back on the bed. But how could she possibly do that with Alex so near? In her heart, she knew they belonged together. But would she ever be able to banish his memories of the woman who'd hurt him so badly?

She sighed deeply. Holly knew she could try. But she wasn't sure yet whether she had the courage to accept what might become of her heart if she failed.

ALEX STOOD IN THE SHADOWS of the hallway, the last light of day throwing the house into a cozy glow. He'd come in from the barn to find the kitchen empty, no cookies baking, no pudding steaming. Then the sound of a piano playing "Jingle Bells" drifted through the house and he had decided to follow it.

He found Eric and Holly in the living room, sitting at the piano that hadn't been played since he'd bought it. Renee had decided she'd get more roles if she knew how to sing and dance, so he'd bought the piano the very same Christmas she'd walked out.

"All right," Holly said. "Now, you play the melody and I'll play the harmony." She counted off the time and they started, then stopped, then started again. Over and over again, she and Eric tried to make it through the song, but at the first mistake, they'd dissolve into peals of laughter.

She never lost her patience with Eric's fumbling attempts, teasing him and tickling him when he'd almost made it through without a mistake and encouraging him when he'd get frustrated. She'd make a wonderful mother, Alex mused. Not just to any man's child, but to *his* child—and the children they could have together.

When they'd finally made it through "Jingle Bells," Holly clapped and cheered for Eric and he stood and took a bow. Then she played a pretty version of "White Christmas," surprising Alex with her skill at the piano. Had she taken lessons as a child? He shook his head. He knew so little about her, about her childhood, about the men in her past, her dreams and goals.

He did know a few important things, though. Holly Bennett was kind and thoughtful, vulnerable yet strong, a woman with an incredible capacity for passion and yet a comforting streak of practicality. He'd grown so accustomed to her little quirks, her need for perfection, that they'd become endearing. All these qualities made up the woman he'd fallen in love with.

"Should we try another?" Holly asked.

"I want you to stay here forever," Eric cried. "You could teach me all kinds of songs."

"That would be nice," Holly said with an indulgent smile. "You'd be a very good pianist in no time at all."

"Will you stay?"

Holly hesitated. "Eric, I have to go back to New York. My job is there. And—and the man I'm going to marry is there."

Eric chewed on his bottom lip. "But couldn't you marry my dad?"

"I don't think your dad is ready to get married again. But someday, I'm sure he will. He'll find the perfect woman and she'll love you and take care of you and you'll be a happy family."

"But you're the perfect woman. You're an angel."

Alex stepped out of the shadows and moved into the room. Eric noticed him first and jumped up from the piano bench. "Dad, Holly taught me to play 'Jingle Bells'! Listen."

He counted off the rhythm and they played the duet flawlessly, Holly embellishing her part until the song sounded like a concerto. When they finished, Alex smiled and clapped and his son beamed.

"We can play it again," Eric said.

Alex chuckled. No doubt he'd be hearing it several times every day until Christmas and long after. "Why don't you wait until your grandfather comes in from the barn," he suggested. "I'm sure he'd like to hear it. In fact, why don't you go down and get him. It's nearly dinnertime. And I need to talk to Holly alone for a minute."

Eric nodded, then ran out of the room. A few moments later, they heard the back door slam and Alex leaned up against the doorjamb, his arms crossed over his chest. "I don't think you should do that," he murmured.

Holly frowned. "I don't understand. You don't want him to play the piano?" She sighed. "I know it's not very macho, but boys take piano lessons, too. In fact, they've found that musical knowledge helps a child in math and—"

"That's not it," Alex said. "I don't think you should let Eric grow so attached to you. He'll only be hurt when you have to leave."

"I haven't done that!" Holly cried. "Just the opposite. But I can't control his feelings. He feels what he wants to feel."

He wasn't the only one, Alex mused. "Well, then find a way to unattach him."

Holly shook her head. "No."

"No?"

"I won't do that. I won't keep him from caring about me. And you can't stop me from loving him. The only way you can is if you tell me to leave. Do you want me to leave?"

"I didn't ask you to come here. We were fine on our own until you showed up."

"Is this about last night?" Holly asked.

"No," he said.

"I thought we understood each other. I came here to do a job and when that's finished, I have to go back to New York. Eric is going to have to learn that people will come into his life, but there's no reason to feel a loss when they leave."

"You weren't here when his mother left. You don't know what he went through."

"I'm not his mother," she said.

"But you could be," Alex countered angrily, "and he knows that."

"Then you have to talk to him. You have to explain."

"You're the one he wants. You're the one I—" He drew a sharp breath. "He won't understand. You're his angel. He thinks you belong to him. To both of us."

"Don't be silly. He knows I have to go back. I told him that."

"He does? Then why was he helping me pick out an engagement ring for you?"

Holly gasped. "What?"

"Last night. We went to Dalton's and he was looking over engagement rings. He got quite an education on cut and clarity."

"I have never asked for an engagement ring!" Holly cried. "And I certainly wouldn't marry you if you offered me one."

"And I don't want to marry you, either!" Alex replied.

"Well, I wouldn't marry you if you paid me a million dollars."

"And if I had a million dollars, I certainly wouldn't pay you to marry me!"

"Why are we screaming at each other?" Holly cried.

"I don't know." He turned away from her, unable to look at her angry eyes and her beautiful face any longer.

He wanted to yank her into his arms and kiss her senseless, to forget the indecision and anxiety that had suddenly invaded their relationship. Why did this have to be so difficult?

"Do you want me to leave?" Holly asked softly.

"No," he said. "That's exactly the point. I don't want you to leave but I don't see how you can stay without hurting Eric." His statement seemed to take her by complete surprise but Alex didn't regret speaking the truth. Couldn't she see how he felt? Wasn't it obvious? Or had he hidden his feelings for such a long time he'd built an invisible wall around his emotions? "Just be careful, all right?"

"All right," she said, her voice cool. "After all, you're the boss." She stood up and started for the kitchen. "Now, if you don't have anything else to discuss, I've got fruitcake to make."

He grabbed her arm as she passed. "I don't like to argue with you," he murmured.

"Then don't," she snapped. "We only have a week until I have to leave. It's silly to spend it shouting at each other."

"And silly to spend it making fruitcake," Alex countered.

"Well, I can't have Christmas without fruitcake. It's perfect for Christmas morning. Toasted. With a cup of good coffee." She walked out of the room toward the kitchen. It was only then that Alex realized they'd solved nothing. They'd begun with a problem and finished with fruitcake and they were both still angry!

He followed her to the kitchen and watched as she pulled ingredients from a grocery bag and tossed them on the counter. She seemed determined to ignore him, refusing to say another word. When she opened a container of nuts, they sprayed all over the counter, but she didn't flinch. Instead she gathered them up and began to neatly chop them into little bits.

"You know, many people have the wrong impression about fruitcake. They think fruitcake is a brick of over-sweet candied fruit that would be better used as a doorstop than a Christmas treat. Well, let me tell you. *Real* fruit-cake has nothing to do with that stuff that's filled with preservatives and pressed by machines into molecular density so high you could use it for ballast on the Titanic. My fruitcake is light and airy and it tastes—perfect!"

"Do we really have to talk about fruitcake?" Alex asked. "I get the feeling you still have a few things to say to me."

"What would you like to talk about? Pfefferneuse? Springerle? Lebkuchen? Baked goods seem to be the only safe subject for us."

"That's not true," Alex said.

"But it should be, because that's what I'm here for. To bake cookies and trim the tree. To spend money on Christ-mas tea towels for the guest bathroom and cinnamon-scented candles for the kitchen. This is what my life has become and the first time that I step outside it and share my feelings with a real family, I get my fingers slapped. So I'll just cream my butter and sift my flour and we'll all be much happier." She wiped her hands on a kitchen towel. "Now, if you'll excuse me, I have a fruitcake to bake."

Alex stood in the kitchen for a long moment, desperate to repair the damage he'd done. He'd never seen Holly quite so hurt. It wasn't that he didn't want her to care about Eric, but he had to protect his son. In the end, he decided to make a quiet retreat. And until he knew precisely what to say to make her feel better, he wasn't going to attempt an apology.

For Alex sensed that he and Holly were teetering on the threshold of something neither one of them were ready for. And he wasn't sure he wanted to be the one to take the first step.

7

THEY'D GONE NEARLY twenty-four hours without speaking, Holly stubbornly refusing to give in and Alex avoiding her at all costs. The tension between them was so thick, she could cut it with a knife, even one of Alex's famously dull kitchen knives! She'd considered an apology, but then decided she'd done nothing wrong. He was angry at her because she was being kind to his son. What did he expect her to do? Though "nice" wasn't part of her contract, she considered it an important quality for a Christmas angel.

Besides, how could she keep from falling in love with Eric Marrin? As for Eric's father, she'd come to regret her earlier good opinion of him. His moods could turn on a dime, from unrestrained desire to cool indifference. She should never have kissed him that day in the sleigh! She should have kept things simple between them.

A thump sounded above her head and Holly jumped. She usually wrote unusual noises off to Eric, but he'd gone outside long ago. She looked up, but nothing was amiss with the ceiling. A series of bumps followed, like footsteps on the roof. Curious, Holly wandered through the house and stepped out onto the front porch. She found a ladder leaning up against the porch roof.

By the time she found a vantage point on the snow-covered front walk, she knew what was up. Alex stood on the porch roof, hefting a huge plastic reindeer up a shorter ladder that lead to the ridgepole of the house. He slipped once and Holly held her breath, pressing her palm to her fluttering heart.

"Be careful," she cried.

He glanced over his shoulder, surprised to see her standing below. "I don't need your advice. I think I can line eight tiny reindeer up without supervision."

"Actually there should be nine. Dasher and Dancer and Prancer and Vixen. Comet and Cupid and Donder and Blitzen. There is some controversy about Donder. Some people call him Donner, but I prefer the traditional Donder. And then there's Rudolph. That's nine." She glanced at the remaining reindeer laying in the snow on their sides. "Nine tacky reindeer," she murmured.

"I'm not putting them up for you, I'm doing it for Eric. So he'll see I can decorate as well as you."

Holly glanced around. "Where is Eric?"

"He went to get an extension cord from the barn."

"That reindeer is too low in the front," she said.

"It's fine," he shouted.

"He looks like he's in a rut," Holly shouted back.

He muttered beneath his breath, just softly enough so Holly couldn't make out the words. No doubt they disparaged her keen sense of perfection. But he did adjust the reindeer so it stood straight. After he fastened the plastic reindeer to the roof, he crawled back down for the next one.

But when he picked it up Holly noticed that it had a red nose. "That's Rudolph," she said. "He's supposed to be first."

"Well, he's going to be second," Alex said.

"Eric will notice. His nose lights up all red like a big old beacon. Everyone will notice Rudolph isn't in the front."

Alex tucked Rudolph under his arm. "Are you here to make my job more miserable, or did you have something to say to me?"

"Actually, I do have something to discuss. I haven't seen any Christmas presents for Eric around the house. Either they're very well hidden or you haven't gotten around to shopping yet." She withdrew a folded sheet of paper from her jeans pocket and held it out to him. "I've made a list of things Eric has mentioned along with a few suggestions for Jed. If you'd like me to shop for you, I can as part of my duties. Of course, there will have to be gifts for Eric from Santa and from you and Jed. And they all have to be wrapped in different paper to maintain the illusion. I've purchased some nice French gift wrap and velvet ribbons and I—"

"I'm sure I can handle it," he said, snatching the list from her fingers. With that, he turned back to the ladder and began to climb up to the porch roof. When he finally settled himself on the peak of the roof, he wrestled Rudolph into the second spot. But the reindeer apparently didn't agree with the choice, because it promptly tipped over on its side and skidded down the roof. When it hit the porch roof it became airborne for a moment before crashing down along the slope and falling off the gutter edge.

Holly had never seen a reindeer truly fly until this moment and she couldn't help but giggle. She stepped back and the reindeer landed a few feet away, headfirst in a snowbank. "Rudolph doesn't take kindly to running behind another reindeer," she shouted.

"Are you personal friends with plastic reindeer?"

She stepped over to the fallen decoration and picked it up. The red nose was cracked and an antler had broken off, but he still seemed to be electrically sound. Holly patted the plastic animal on the head, then sat down on the front steps, Rudolph beside her. As expected, Alex joined her a few moments later.

"So, when do you plan to shop?" Holly asked. "Some of the toys on the list might be sold out if you don't go soon."

Alex hooked his thumbs in the back pockets of his jeans and stared down at her. "I think I can handle Christmas shopping for my son. I know what he likes."

"I was just trying to help," she said. "That's what I'm here for."

"And how much longer will you be here?" Alex asked. "I know you're supposed to stay until Christmas Day, but I'm sure you're anxious to get back. Your fiancé must want you home for the holidays, doesn't he?"

Holly frowned. "My fiancé?"

"Yeah, the guy you're supposed to marry?" He paused. "I heard you mention him again when you were talking to Eric."

"You were listening?"

"He's my son. I have to protect him. I've been thinking if you stay for the holidays, it might send the wrong message. And it might be harder for him when you leave."

"I would never deliberately hurt him," Holly murmured.

"Every day you're here he becomes more attached. You know that."

Holly's anger rose anew. Why was she being punished for feelings she had no control over? "Then I'll leave," she said. "I'll finish my work this week. I can prepare your Christmas dinner early and you can simply reheat it. I'll be out of here by Friday or Saturday afternoon at the latest."

To her surprise, he didn't try to convince her to stay.

Instead he nodded curtly, then made to go back to work on the rooftop. But before he climbed the ladder, he turned back to her. "Do you love him?" Alex asked.

"Eric? Of course, I love him. Who wouldn't? He's a wonderful boy and you should be very proud."

His stony expression cracked for a moment. "No," he murmured. "I meant your fiancé."

Holly shrugged as she considered her answer. She knew the truth, but she found in the lie a way to protect her heart, to exact a little revenge for his boorish behavior. "I suppose I do." She smiled smugly. "He asked me to marry him and he's the only offer I've had."

He kicked a clod of snow with the toe of his boot, avoiding her eyes. "Well, then I guess you should marry him."

"Yes, I guess I should," she murmured. Holly slowly stood, then forced a smile. He'd made his feelings perfectly clear. There was no future here for her. The wonderful days they'd spent falling in love were in the past. Her time at Stony Creek Farm was as she always knew it to be—a job and nothing more. "Well, I suppose I'd better finish the rest of the decorating in the next couple of days. I've got shopping and cooking to do. Do you have any requests for dinner on Christmas Eve and Christmas Day?"

He shook his head. "Whatever you suggest will be fine."

His voice was cool, indifferent, and she wondered how he could simply forget what they'd shared. She shoved the reindeer at him then hurried inside the house.

When she reached the solitude of the kitchen, she braced her hands on the edge of the counter and drew a calming breath. "Just do the job," she said. "Just do the job and everything will be all right."

With a silent oath, she yanked open cabinet doors and began to pull out ingredients. She'd make the best Christmas meals she'd ever made—Beef Wellington for Christmas Eve, and a plump roast turkey for Christmas Day, with all the trimmings, so tasty that he'd moan with pleasure and regret ever sending her away.

She grabbed a bag of cornmeal and tore it open. First she'd make corn bread for the turkey stuffing. And then she'd prepare the brioche pastry for the Beef Wellington. And after that, she'd put the final touches on her decorations, making the house shine like something out of the December issue of *House Beautiful.*

"I'll make him sorry he sent me packing," Holly muttered. "One taste of my sausage and cornmeal dressing and he'll never forget me."

"BUT YOU HAVE TO COME!" Eric cried. "It's my holiday pageant. I'm going to play the bells along with "Santa Claus is Comin' to Town." It's the most important part. Miss Green said so. And—and Eleanor Winchell is playing Mrs. Santa Claus and she looks just like a big red tomato with legs in her costume."

Alex stood behind his son, his hands on Eric's shoulders. He'd tried to convince him that Holly had too much work to do, but Eric could not be swayed. "Holly's been working really hard, Scout. Maybe she'd like a little time to herself."

"I do have a lot of work to do," Holly murmured, though Alex couldn't imagine what was left to be done. The house looked like a page out of some glossy magazine, every detail perfect. She'd been cooking up a storm in the kitchen, and though he'd generally been absent from the house, he could smell the results of her efforts every evening when he came in from the stables.

She glanced across the room at him and her gaze lingered for a long moment. He'd changed from his usual dress of jeans and flannel work shirt into a wool jacket and finely pressed khakis. He'd even taken care with his hair, using a comb instead of his fingers, and had exchanged his comfortable work boots for fashionable loafers. Though he might not be as sophisticated as her "fiancé", some women found him attractive.

Alex met her gaze, trying to read her expression. At first he'd thought nothing of pushing her away. After all, she didn't really care. But lately, whenever they glanced at each other, he saw a tiny flicker of hurt in her expression, as if she were trying to maintain her composure but fighting her emotions.

"We really would like you to come," Alex said. Though the invitation was genuine, his voice sounded forced.

They'd shared only polite conversation over the past four days, a word here, a comment there. In truth, they behaved precisely as he might have expected when she arrived, maintaining a cordial business relationship and a careful distance. She had stopped eating dinners at the house, fixing her own in the little kitchenette in her room.

Every evening, she and Eric would tackle another craft project for the holidays and he'd excuse himself to go to the barn, only returning to the house after he saw the lights in the tack house go on. And when Eric had asked her to take him shopping for Christmas presents, she'd passed the job off to his grandfather.

Alex should have been happy. After all, he was the one who suggested she put some distance between herself and Eric. But in truth, the atmosphere around the house was anything but festive. A depressing gloom now seemed to hang over them, Holly on one side of a dark cloud of confusion and he and Eric on the other. And all of them anticipating the day she'd leave with varying emotions.

Holly placed her hand on the top of Eric's head and looked down at him. "I really would like to come, but I just can't take the time away. I've got pies to bake and peanut brittle to make. You want a perfect Christmas, don't you?"

Alex cleared his throat. "Eric, go get your jacket. And put your boots on over your good shoes. We have to leave in a few minutes."

When he left the room, Alex turned back to Holly. "I do want you to come. It would make Eric so happy."

"Are you asking me to come along for Eric? Or because you want me to?"

"Both," he said. "I'd like you to be there."

Holly considered the invitation for a long moment, then nodded. "All right. I'll go. Should I change?"

"You look nice the way you are," he said. She was dressed in a pretty celery-green sweater set and a black corduroy skirt that showed off her long legs. Her pale hair was pulled back in a pretty patterned scarf and she wore just enough makeup to highlight her incredible beauty. In his eyes, she was perfect.

He held out his hand. "Come on. We don't want to be late for Eric's big debut."

Holly grabbed her jacket from the back of a kitchen stool and began to tug it on. But Alex took it from her hands and held it out behind her. "I appreciate this."

She didn't say another word, all the way to school, sitting on the far side of the truck, when he helped her back out of her coat in the lobby, even when he slipped her hand into the crook of his arm as they walked toward the gymnasium. She simply smiled woodenly and stared straight ahead. So much was left unsaid between them, neither one of them wanting to venture into territory better left undisturbed.

How many times had he fought the urge to pull her into his arms, to say all the things he'd been thinking about the two of them, to put things back the way they were, so full of warmth and excitement? But when he opened his mouth, doubts rushed up to drown his resolve. He didn't want to make another mistake. Divorcing Renee had been bad enough, but to love then lose Holly would tear his heart in two. And it might destroy what was left of Eric's trust as well.

As they walked into the dimly lit gym, Alex watched every head turn to stare at them. The status of his social life had been a matter of some curiosity around town. Behind the suave and wealthy Thomas Dalton, president of Dalton's Department Store, Alex Marrin was considered quite the catch for Schuyler Falls' single women. And now, without warning, he suddenly appeared with a beautiful woman on his arm, and to a school function at that!

"Why are they staring?" Holly murmured.

Alex gave her hand a squeeze. "They're staring at you."

"Why?"

"This is the first time I've been out in public with a woman since Eric's mother walked out."

"You haven't had a date in two years?" she asked. "Why not?"

"I guess I hadn't really found anyone I wanted to date—until you."

"This is not a date," she snapped.

Alex grinned ruefully. "Can we pretend it is? It'll put all the matchmaking mothers off my scent for a while. You wouldn't have to kiss me. Just look at me adoringly every now and then and act like every word I say is the most fascinating thing you ever heard.''

This brought a tiny giggle and Alex felt the tension between them crumble a bit. ''And what happens when you go out in public the next time?'' she asked.

He shrugged. ''Rent a date? 1-800-HOT-BABE? Or maybe I just won't go out again for a year or two.''

Alex wove his fingers through hers as they made their way to their seats, finding a spot in the middle of a row not far from the front. When they settled, he handed her a program. ''I know you probably haven't ever been to a school pageant, but I think I should give you a few tips.''

''What kind of tips?''

''No matter how bad it is, don't laugh. You can smile, but you can't laugh. I find that biting the inside of my bottom lip can be helpful. Believe me, it's going to be really bad. Children this age are incapable of standing in front of a crowd of people and acting normal. And Miss Green's second-grade class won't be driving the Vienna Boys Choir out of business anytime soon. Their singing closely resembles shouting.''

''I'm sure I'll enjoy every minute,'' Holly said.

When the gymnasium was nearly full, the lights dimmed even further and the murmur from the crowd quieted. The pageant began with the first-grade students. Almost on cue, as the music teacher raised her arms to conduct, video cameras began to whir and flashes popped. The children barely paid attention to their song, preferring instead to search the audience for their parents, bother the student standing next to them, or find an original way to play with their clothes. Thankfully the first-graders only did one song before scurrying off the stage.

Eric's class came on next. Holly reached out and took Alex's hand, giving it an encouraging squeeze. He glanced at her and found her gnawing at her bottom lip. "Are you all right?"

"I'm really nervous for him," she said. "He's been talking about this solo all week and I think he's really worried he'll mess up."

"Eric doesn't get nervous," Alex said.

"Yes, he does. He doesn't say anything, but I know how much he wants to do well."

Alex sat back in his chair, pondering Holly's keen insight into his son as he stared down at her delicate fingers. He'd always thought of Eric as such a confident kid, jumping into every situation with careless abandon, then shrugging off any failures as if they didn't matter in the least. He'd never considered that Eric might be hiding his fears and insecurities, living up to an ideal of masculinity that he saw in his father. A mother would notice these things—if Eric had a mother to raise him.

He stole another glance at Holly. She'd make a wonderful mother. Even now, she sat on the edge of her seat, awaiting Eric's big moment in the spotlight, her smile tight, her shoulders tense. She loved his son and admitted that freely. With a woman like Holly, maybe Eric might experience the softer side of life, the side filled with hugs when he felt scared and kisses when he cried.

"There he is," Holly murmured, pointing to the far end of the group. She waved as Eric scanned the crowd and when he saw them both, he beamed with a wide grin. "We should have brought a camera. He looks so sweet, doesn't he?"

Eric and the rest of the little orchestra wore jaunty Santa hats and stood at a table, their bells spread in front of them. As the song began, they raised their mallets and the harmonies chimed out along with the vocals. Eric's face was set in fierce concentration as he played.

Suddenly he lost his place and looked up at the teacher hopelessly, chewing on the rubber mallet nervously. Alex heard Holly draw a sharp breath and she nearly broke his fingers clenching his hand. But then the music teacher nodded at Eric and he joined back in. Holly relaxed, releasing her tightly held breath. And when it was all over, she jumped to her feet and clapped.

"Bravo!" she cried, beaming at Eric and waving.

Alex glanced around to find the rest of the parents staring at her and he grabbed Holly by the arm and tugged her back down in her chair. "This isn't Lincoln Center," he whispered over the polite applause. "There won't be any encores."

Her smile was exuberant and her eyes were bright with pride. "Didn't he do well? I think he lost his place for a moment, but then he joined right back in. He had such composure. I think he had the most notes to play, don't you?"

Alex couldn't resist. He slipped his arm around her shoulders and pulled her closer. "I haven't seen you this excited since you found that moldy thing for the pudding."

A pretty blush stained her cheeks and she averted her gaze. "I'm sorry, I shouldn't have—"

"No," Alex interrupted. "It's nice that you care so much."

The rest of the program passed slowly, each grade level playing two songs for the audience before filing off the choir risers. The evening ended with the entire school and audience joining in a rousing chorus of "We Wish You A Merry Christmas," complete with a figgy pudding verse.

They met Eric in the hallway outside his classroom. He bounded up to them, anxious to gather compliments for his performance. Alex gave him a gruff hug and ruffled his hair. "You were great," he said.

Then Holly bent down and took Eric's hands. "It was so wonderful," she said. "You played so well and I could hear your bell all the way to where we were sitting. You were definitely the best."

"I messed up a little," he admitted.

"I hardly noticed. And I don't think anyone in the audience could tell. I think they were all so caught up in the beautiful music and the singing. It was very professional."

"Really?" Eric asked. "Like something you would see in New York?"

"Absolutely," Holly replied. "Better than what I've seen in New York."

She took his hand and they started toward the front door of the school. Alex stood in the hallway watching the two of them together, his son and the woman he was fast falling in love with. He raked his hands through his hair, then slowly shook his head.

"Well, Marrin. If you really love her, then I guess you're going to have to find some way to convince her to stay." He took a deep breath, then started after them. "Either that, or risk the wrath of an angry seven-year-old."

HOLLY LAY ON HER BED in the tack house, staring up at the ceiling, her hands folded over her chest. To say she was confused was an understatement. Alex Marrin had become the master of mixed signals. First, he wanted her to stay. Then he wanted her to go. And now, she wasn't sure what he wanted.

After they'd returned home from Eric's pageant, she'd excused herself to go back to the tack house. But he'd grabbed her hand and asked if she'd like to join him and Eric for hot cocoa and cookies before the night ended. They'd popped in *How The Grinch Stole Christmas* and sat around a fire in the family room, reliving the highlights of the evening and laughing along to Dr. Seuss.

And when Eric finally wandered off to bed, Alex had joined her on the sofa. But instead of letting the evening spin out in front of them, she panicked and jumped up, mumbling some feeble excuse about calling Meg before it was too late. Then she made a hasty exit and closed herself safely in her room where she found some solitude to think.

What had she been so afraid of? That Alex might just kiss her and start everything all over again between them? In her present state of mind, she could just about walk away without shattering into a million pieces. She still had a chance of going back to her life in New York and putting her time at Stony Creek Farm in the past.

But how would he feel? Was she giving up on them too soon? Her contemplation of Alex Marrin's sudden turnabout was interrupted by a knock on her bedroom door. She glanced over at the clock at her bedside. It was past eleven. There was only one person who would come knocking at such a late hour and Holly wasn't sure she wanted to answer.

He knocked again and Holly covered her eyes, willing him to go back to the house and make her life simple again. But when he knocked for the third time, she sighed and rolled off the bed. She pulled the door open to find Alex standing on the other side, bags and boxes piled so high in his arms that she could barely see him.

"I saw your light on," he said from the other side of a huge Lego set. "I—I thought I'd bring these down."

Holly grabbed the top of the stack, uncovering his head

and shoulders. Their gazes met and she felt a shiver skitter down her spine. Why was he doing this to her? Weren't things already settled between them?

"You said you'd wrap them and I wanted to get them done before Eric finds them and knows what I'm getting him. I'm going to hide them in the loft above the other bedroom. I don't think he'll find them there." He set the rest of the presents on the bed, then stepped back, rubbing his hands together. "I went a little nuts."

Holly stared at the pile of toys and sighed. "I guess I could work on these tomorrow morning before I leave."

"You're leaving tomorrow?" Alex asked. Then he nodded, drawing a sharp breath. "That's right. Tomorrow."

"I thought I would. Saturday is Christmas Eve and the train will be packed with travellers. I wanted to get an early start."

Alex nodded silently. "I guess that would be best."

"Yes," she said.

The conversation between them faded and they stood watching each other uneasily. Holly waited for him to leave, to make some silly excuse and walk away. But in the end, he muttered a soft curse, crossed the space between them in two long steps and pulled her into his arms.

A tiny cry slipped from her lips as he brought his mouth down on hers, more a surprise than a protest. She'd tried so hard to commit the taste of him to memory, but nothing prepared her for the sheer intensity of his kiss. His tongue teased hers, first gently, then demanding her unfettered response.

Holly moaned softly as her knees went weak. His hands spanning her waist, Alex slowly pushed her back toward the bed. When the edge hit her knees, he stopped and reached around her, sending toys and boxes and bags flying across the room. Then, he gently pushed her down and lowered himself to lie beside her.

His hand skimmed along the front of her cashmere cardigan then splayed on her belly, softly massaging her waist as he kissed her again. "I'm sorry," he murmured, his breath warm against her mouth. "I've made such a mess of things."

"No," she said, pressing her finger to his lips. "No apologies. This is all that matters. Just this night. I don't need any more than this."

"Holly, I need to tell you—"

She cut off his words with a kiss, furrowing her fingers into his hair at his nape and pulling his mouth down on hers. He grabbed her hips and rolled her over on top of him, settling her against his body, his broad chest and lean, long legs.

Every shred of common sense she still possessed told her to stop before they went too far. But her common sense was silenced by her need—for his taste, his touch, his smell. His fingers wove through her hair, pulling it down around them like a curtain of flax, shutting out the world and the past.

With every breath, Holly sank further into the magic of the moment, the pure sensation of his touch, the warmth of his body. A hunger to possess him surged up inside of her, but she didn't feel the urgency she felt that night in the stable. Tonight, they had all the time in the world.

Slowly his hands explored her body, toying with the buttons of her sweater before moving on. But when his hands skimmed beneath the cashmere to cup her breasts, Holly moaned, arching her back and bracing her hands on either side of his head. She pushed away from him and stood beside the bed. Alex watched her through passion-glazed eyes, his elbows cocked behind him.

A tiny smile curled the corners of Holly's mouth as she reached for the top button of her sweater. She flipped it open and Alex sent her a devilish grin. Another button followed and he growled playfully. When she finally finished, he made a move to join her, but Holly held up her hand, warning him to stay where he was.

She toyed with him, letting the sweater fall off her shoulders and feeling for the first time the power of her femininity. With just a casual smile or a suggestive movement, she could pique his desire, make him feel a need so powerful he ached to touch her. No man had ever wanted her more than Alex did. She could see it in the way his gaze caressed her body, taking in every detail with a lazy appreciation.

When she reached for the clasp at the front of her bra, Alex shook his head. "No," he murmured. Slowly he rose from the bed to stand in front of her, his head bent. "Let me."

His fingers dipped between the soft swells of her breasts and with a careless flick, her bra fell open. She wasn't embarrassed by her nakedness, but emboldened. She reached for his jacket and tugged it off, then set to work on his shirt. Piece by piece, the fabric barriers dropped until he stood before her, bare-chested. He gently drew her into his arms and skin met skin, the heat from his body seeping into hers in a delicious rush.

As if they existed in another world, a world of endless nights, they slowly peeled the rest of their clothing off of each other. Every movement gave time to tease, to explore, to tantalize until Holly couldn't deny the passion that swelled inside of her. When they were both naked, she took a step back and looked at him, so strong and yet strangely vulnerable. At that moment, Holly knew he was all the man she'd ever want.

They tumbled back onto the bed together, limbs tangling, skin tingling. Soft moans mixed with urgent whispers and Holly's senses whirled with the heady scent of him, the damp of his tongue on her nipple and the harsh sound of his breathing. No words were needed between them and when he retrieved a foil packet from his wallet, Holly took it from him and quickly sheathed him.

They seemed to respond to each other instinctively, as if they'd always been meant to reach this moment in time, this instant when his body became one with hers. And as he entered her, his hips sinking against hers, Holly looked up at him. All the emotion was there in his eyes, the unspoken love, the undeniable need, and every nerve in her body sang.

She didn't need to hear that he loved her, for she knew it in her heart. And if he never uttered the words aloud, never acknowledged his feelings, she still knew that, for a single night, she was the woman of his dreams. Holly reached out and cupped his cheek in her palm. He pressed a kiss there, then closed his eyes.

He moved slowly at first, but then uncontrollable desire took hold of them both. Deep in her core, Holly felt the tension grow with each thrust, a strange compelling need that begged to be satisfied. And when he slipped his hand between their bodies to touch her, she cried out with the intensity of the sensation, falling headlong into her release. Alex followed her, calling out her name again and again as he came inside of her.

And later, after they'd made love once again and he lay beside her, Holly reached out to touch his face. As a young girl, she'd had dreams of meeting a man she could truly and deeply love, with fierce passion and utter stillness. But as she grew older, she'd given up those dreams for a more pragmatic approach to love, never realizing the woman she really was inside. With Alex, she'd become more than she'd ever been, a woman filled with light and life and a love that overcame all her doubts and inhibitions.

"I love you," she murmured, so softly that, if he did hear, he'd think it was only a dream. "And if this is the only night we have between us, I'll still love you." She placed a kiss on her fingertips, then touched his parted lips. Holly watched him for a long time, her eyes growing heavy with sleep. And when she finally drifted off, his head nestled against her shoulder, her sleep was deep and dreamless.

8

THE SUN WAS STILL FAR below the horizon when Alex opened his eyes. He drew a deep breath, taking in the sweet scent of Holly's hair. Sometime during the night, he'd tucked her against his body, her backside nestled in his lap, his arms wrapped around her waist. She fit so perfectly against his body, as if they were meant to begin and end the day together just like this.

When he'd brought the pile of presents to her room, he never thought they'd end up in bed. He just wanted to see her face one more time before he went to sleep, needed to assure himself that she was there. But, somehow, the tension between them dissolved completely and the inevitable came to pass. Hell, it had been so long, he'd wondered whether he still knew how to please a woman.

His thoughts wandered back to the moment when he'd moved inside of her, to the single shattering second when she arched beneath him and found her release. Perfection, he mused. He'd never made love so completely, so intensely. The very act seemed to seal a trust between them that couldn't be broken.

Alex glanced over at the clock on the nightstand: 5:00 a.m. Jed would be up and around soon, ready to get to work in the barn. If he slipped out now, he'd be able to change into his work clothes and make it to the barn without any unanswerable questions from his father. But the bed was warm and Holly's body soft, and he'd be crazy to leave.

What a change. He'd been a fool up until the moment he'd kissed her last night, determined to develop some immunity to her charms, convinced that she'd hurt him like Renee had. But he was older now and much wiser. And he didn't look at Holly through a veil of boyish exuberance and innocence. He saw her as she really was— as a woman he could spend a lifetime loving.

He picked up a strand of her hair and brushed it against his chin, wondering what the morning would bring. Would she regret what had happened or would she realize her future was with him? Alex pressed a kiss against the curve of her shoulder. She stirred slightly, then sighed and fell back into a deep sleep.

He had no right to expect anything from her. What had she said? No promises? He'd vowed never to make promises to a woman again. But the prospect of promising to love and honor—hell, even to obey—didn't seem so unnerving, not when the woman standing with him at the altar was Holly.

He slowly sat up, pulling his arm from beneath her and shaking it to restore circulation. The chill air of the bedroom sent a shiver over his naked chest and he reached over to tug the quilt up over her bare skin, allowing his fingers to linger just a little longer. He fought the temptation to wake her and make love to her again. They'd only fallen asleep a few hours before. He and Holly had a lot to talk about when she woke up and he needed her to be well-rested.

He crawled out of bed and began to search the room for his clothes, tugging them on as he found them. Embers from a fire he'd built for them both, glowed among the ashes, providing just enough light to see. When Alex was finally dressed, he crossed back to the bed and squatted down beside Holly.

He smoothed a strand of hair from her eyes and his gaze skimmed her peaceful features. She'd never been more beautiful to him than at that moment, not because they'd just made love, but because he realized that she was the woman he loved.

"Hey," he murmured. "Wake up, sweetheart."

Her eyes fluttered, then opened, and she smiled at him sleepily. "Why are you leaving? Is everything all right? Is it Eric?"

"No," he said, brushing a kiss along her lips. "I need to get back to the house. Jed will be up soon and then Eric. I'm always there when Eric gets up."

"Mmm," she said, snuggling further under the covers. "Will you come back after he goes to school?"

"I promise," Alex replied. "If you promise you won't move until I get back."

"I promise."

This time he kissed her long and deep, before dragging himself away. "I'll be back," he murmured. Reluctantly, Alex closed the door behind him, then hurried back to the house, the cold air clearing his head with the swiftness of a sledgehammer. The kitchen was dark when he walked through, heading straight for the coffeemaker.

"You're up early."

The sound of Jed's voice startled him. He glanced over his shoulder and watched as his father strolled into the kitchen. Jed was already dressed, but hadn't bothered to shave that morning. He pushed Alex aside and started to make coffee, filling the pot with water and dumping coffee into the filter.

"Or maybe you haven't been to bed yet," Jed said. He

gave Alex the once-over, then chuckled. "Aren't those the same clothes you were wearing last night?"

"What are you? Chief of the fashion police? You've never noticed before when I've worn the same clothes two days in a row."

"Those aren't your work clothes." He stuck his coffee mug under the stream of fresh coffee, filled it half full, then exchanged it with the pot. "And, there was never a beautiful woman staying in the tack house before." Jed took a slow sip of his coffee as he stared shrewdly at Alex over the rim of his mug. When he set the mug down, he sighed. "You want her to stay, don't you?"

Alex ran his hand through his hair. "Yeah, I guess I do." He cursed softly. "But I'm afraid to ask her."

"Why?"

"Because I'm afraid she'll refuse. Or even worse, I'm afraid she'll accept. And then I'll screw it up all over again, the same way I did with Renee."

"Son, you didn't mess up with Renee. You did everything you could to hold that marriage together. How many other men would let their wives live in New York half the days of the year? She was the wrong woman for you. Maybe now, you've found the right one."

"I thought Renee was the right one."

"No, you thought Renee was glamorous and exciting and sophisticated. You were starstruck. And Renee thought you were rich enough to finance her acting career. She was selfish. If she hadn't gotten pregnant two months after the wedding, you probably wouldn't have lasted a year."

"So that only proves I've got rotten judgment when it comes to women. Up until this moment, I actually believed Renee married me because she loved me. Thanks for the insight, Dad."

His sarcasm wasn't lost on Jed. The old man chuckled. "That's what I'm here for."

Alex raked his fingers through his hair again and pressed the heels of his hands against his temples. "How the hell am I supposed to know how I feel? I've known Holly for two weeks, give or take a few days. I don't know anything about her family, I don't know what perfume she likes, what her favorite color is."

"There are a lot of things you *do* know."

"I don't know whether she'd want to live here, on a horse farm in upstate New York. She's a city girl. Her friends are there, her career. What is she going to do on this farm?"

"You know what's in your heart, Alex. That's all you really need to know."

"What about what's in *her* heart?"

"Well, that you won't know until you ask her. But I can tell you this, if you let her leave without telling her how you feel, you'll always wonder." Jed rubbed his chin. "Wait here. I have something that might help you decide."

He hurried off into the dark of the house while Alex poured himself a mug of coffee. If only he had more time with Holly. A month or two. Maybe a little more. Then he could rid himself of the last traces of doubt. Hell, everything seemed so simple, lying in bed with Holly in his arms. But in the growing light of day, it wasn't easy at all. After just two weeks, planning a future with Holly was a big gamble. He'd lost the gamble once and he was loathe to take the risk again.

But if he didn't take the risk, what kind of future was he making for himself? A long life of solitude, a cold bed and an empty heart. Raising a son without a mother.

Never filling the house with all the children he once wanted to have.

Alex smiled. Holly would give him beautiful children. Perhaps a little girl with pretty green eyes and golden hair. And a little brother for Eric. If only Holly would stay, his life might mean something again.

"I've wanted to give this to you for a while," Jed said as he came back into the kitchen. "But I thought it might not be the right time. Here," he said, handing Alex a tiny velvet bag.

Alex loosened the drawstring and tipped the bag upside down over his palm. A ring fell out, a large diamond in an antique platinum setting. "Mother wore this," Alex said. "I remember."

Jed nodded. "And your grandmother. And your great-grandmother. Your wife should wear it, don't you think?"

"Renee was my—"

"I didn't think she deserved it," Jed said. "As it turns out, I was right. But I think that ring would look mighty pretty on Holly's finger."

Alex shook his head. "Marriage. That's a big step. I'm not ready to jump into that mess again. And I'm certainly not going to ask Holly after just two weeks together." He held the ring between his fingers. It would look beautiful on Holly, slipped over her slender finger. Holly loved tradition and old things.

"You're a Marrin. It's not supposed to take time. If she's the one, then you need to ask her."

"I think that family tradition ought to stop with my generation. I have to think of Eric, too." He glanced up at Jed. "What if things don't work out? He was so hurt when Renee left. I don't want him hurt again. Not like that."

Jed rested his hand on Alex's shoulder. "Don't waste

too much time chewing on this, son. If you let her leave, you might never get her back.''

His father grabbed his mug of coffee and his jacket from the back of a chair and slipped out of the house, leaving Alex to contemplate his choices. But no matter how he looked at his situation, he couldn't come up with a logical plan.

Maybe love wasn't supposed to be logical, Alex mused. Maybe it was supposed to be crazy and irrational, driving a man to distraction. It was all so much easier when he was younger, the choices so clear, the consequences still unknown.

He placed the ring back in the velvet bag, then wandered upstairs to his bedroom. He caught a glimpse of himself in the mirror above his dresser. His eyes were bleary and his hair still tousled by her fingers. But there was something there that hadn't been before—a peace, a calm, as if he'd finally found a center to his life.

Now, if he could only make it last.

''HOLLY! HOLLY, ARE YOU HERE?''

Holly slowly opened her eyes. She rolled over to find the bed empty, the spot where Alex had spent the night no longer occupied. He'd gone sometime before sunrise, leaving her to catch up on all the sleep she'd missed. Holly smiled, then pulled the covers up to her chin. She felt relaxed, completely sated—she took a peek under the covers—and completely naughty. She couldn't remember ever sleeping naked.

''Holly, it's me. Eric.'' A soft rap sounded at the door. ''Can I come in?''

She sat up in bed, knowing that Alex hadn't locked the door behind him. It could only be locked from the inside. ''Wait a minute!'' she called. ''Just let me get dressed.''

Leaping from the warm bed, Holly searched the room for anything to wear. She tugged on the sweater she'd worn the night before, then yanked on the bottoms of her new flannel pajamas. Christmas presents were still scattered all over the room. With the expertise of a professional soccer player, she kicked them under the bed.

The doorknob turned. "Are you awake? Can I come in?"

She raced back to the bed and grabbed a Widgie Midget miniature toy robot and shoved it under her sweater. Then she casually sat down on the edge of the bed. An instant later, Eric threw the door open and raced inside, a long florist's box in his arms. He stumbled as he neared the bed and the box went flying, falling open on the patchwork quilt. "Holly, look! You got flowers! They just brought them. And they're not even plastic!"

Eric crawled up on the bed and carefully scrutinized the flowers from close range. "I think they're roses."

"Alex," Holly murmured. She wrapped her arms around herself and sighed. What a wonderful way to start the day, she mused. A bleep and blurp sounded from beneath her sweater and she remembered the little robot she had hidden there.

"What was that?" Eric asked.

"Just my tummy," Holly replied. "I guess I'm a little hungry."

Eric frowned in confusion. "My tummy never makes sounds like that, even when I'm starving."

"Good morning."

They both looked up and saw Alex standing in the doorway. He was dressed in his work clothes, his hair windblown and flecked with chaff, his arms spread across the width of the doorjamb. Eric bounced up and down on the bed and pointed to the roses. "Dad, look at what Holly got. Flowers."

For a long moment, their gazes locked and memories of the night before came flooding back, the frantic need, the ache to touch him, and the final surrender. Holly felt her face warm with a blush and she wondered how long it would be before they shared a bed again. Would he come to her tonight? Or would they steal some time together during the daylight hours? "Thank you," she said, sending him a silent smile of gratitude.

Alex shrugged. "You're very welcome. But if you're thanking me for the flowers, I didn't send them."

She blinked, then glanced down at the roses scattered across the bed. "Then who did?" Holly asked. "Who would send me two dozen roses?" She gently tickled Eric's knee. "Did you send me flowers?"

"Maybe there's a card," Alex suggested, stepping into the room, now curious himself.

Eric rummaged through the box and came up with a small envelope. "Here it is. Should I read it?"

"If you can," Holly said.

He pulled the card from the envelope and scrunched his face as he looked at it. "Merry Christmas. Call me. Love—Step—Step—Hand. Who is Step-Hand?"

Holly snatched the card from Eric's fingers, gasping when she re-read the inscription. "Stephan?" she breathed. The robot squeaked from beneath her sweater again, causing a giggle from Eric. "But—I don't understand. Why would he—" She snapped her mouth shut. Could he have changed his mind about marrying that other woman?

"Who's Stephan?" Eric asked.

Alex took another step toward the bed. "Eric, go help

your grandfather in the barn. He's working in Emmy's stall.''

"But Holly is—"

"Eric, do as I say. Now.'' His voice had suddenly chilled and his expression grew hard. The boy saw the change on his father's face and knew not to argue any further. He sighed dramatically, then clomped out of the room, shooting Alex a perturbed look as he passed.

An uneasy silence began the moment the door clicked shut. Holly flicked the card with her finger and tried to avoid Alex's penetrating gaze. And Alex stood silently near the bed, waiting for some explanation.

In truth, Holly had none. She couldn't imagine why Stephan would send her flowers—especially now. Unless…she swallowed hard. Unless he wanted her back. "This doesn't make any sense,'' she murmured, forcing a smile.

"I agree. Flowers from a fiancé. What are the odds?''

Holly cursed beneath her breath. "I don't have a fiancé! I mean, I could have had a fiancé, but when he asked, I told him I needed time to think. And—and I just never got back to him with an answer. And then he got engaged to someone else and I just assumed it was over between us.''

"So when you told me you were engaged, that was a—''

"A slight exaggeration,'' Holly admitted. She groaned. "All right, it was a lie. But I had my reasons.''

"Well, he's obviously changed his mind.''

"No! He couldn't have. He's getting married in the Hamptons in June. I haven't spoken to him in nearly a year. He didn't even know I was here!'' Holly cried.

"Do you love him?''

"No!'' Holly cried, stunned that he'd ask her such a

question. "Do you think I would have made love to you if I still loved him?"

"I don't know you well enough to know what you'd do," Alex muttered.

"He can't possibly believe I'd still want to marry him. I—I said no!" She winced. "Or at least I should have. Since I didn't give him an answer, wouldn't you think he'd interpret that as a no?"

"I wouldn't," Alex said. He shook his head. "When you told me you were engaged, I didn't really believe you. I just thought you were saying that because you wanted to protect your virtue."

She stared at the card, baffled. "Well, we both know how safe my virtue was with you."

Though Holly hadn't meant to be hurtful, Alex caught the hint of regret in her voice. "Holly, there were two of us in this room last night. Neither of us wanted to stop." He crossed the room to the bed, gathered up the flowers and tossed them on the floor. Then he sat down beside her and took her face between his hands. "Forget him. He's been out of your life for a year. What we have is real and it's happening now." He wove his fingers through hers. "Holly, I want you to stay. Not just for Christmas, but forever."

His words didn't register at first, unable to penetrate her preoccupation with the roses. Something wasn't right here. Stephan was engaged, to a woman with money. He'd never give that up for Holly. And he certainly wasn't the type to send flowers. "I—I should call him," she said.

"No," Alex replied. "You don't have to call him. Holly, listen." He tipped her chin up until she met his gaze. "I need you. Eric needs you. And I want you to stay."

Her eyes went wide and she blinked, finally hearing his

haphazard proposal. "You want me to stay? But—but I thought you weren't ready to—"

He reached out and cupped her cheek in his hand, stopping her words. "I know I haven't made my feelings very clear, but I know this much—I'm in love with you, Holly, and I want you to be a part of our lives."

Holly wasn't sure what to say. Though she'd dreamed about a future with Alex and Eric, she never thought it would come to be. In truth, she'd convinced herself it was an impossibility! But this wasn't a real future he offered. In truth, he hadn't made any more promises than he had earlier.

What could she expect? They barely knew each other. A marriage proposal would be foolish at such an early stage, especially considering Alex's track record. But could she give up her life and her career in New York for the mere possibility of a life with Eric and Alex? Could she become a lover to Alex and a mother to Eric without knowing the future? And though she'd come to recognize her potential as a parent, taking on that responsibility fulltime was another matter. What if she wasn't a good mother? What if she made mistakes and messed up Eric's life? Alex would never forgive her.

And then there was Alex. Though she'd fallen in love with him, she still barely knew him. What if his feelings faded? What if he realized later he'd made a mistake in asking her to stay? Could her heart take the pain of leaving both Alex and Eric after becoming a part of their family for real?

"Aren't you going to give me an answer?" he asked.

"This isn't a marriage proposal, is it," she said.

Alex's jaw grew tight, his eyes hard. "You know my track record with that."

Holly frowned. "I—I'm not sure. I'll have to think about it. We'll have to talk about it."

Alex cursed. "Like you thought about the other guy's proposal? Ignoring it for a year while you hoped it would go away? I'm not going away so easily. I want an answer now."

Holly drew a deep breath, regret filling her expression. "My answer is I can't give you an answer now. There are just so many things I have to consider."

"Then last night meant nothing to you?"

"Alex, last night was wonderful. I've never felt such…passion. But it's just a beginning. I can't change my whole life based on one wonderful night in bed. Even if it *was* really good. I'm a practical person. If you really knew me, then you'd understand." She picked up a rose from the floor and stared at it, frowning. "And as much as I'd love to accept, I'm obviously not free to do that right now. I have to go back and give Stephan an answer. Until I do that, I can't give *you* an answer."

Alex stood, anger evident in his expression. "I should have known. I should have trusted my instincts," he muttered. He stalked to the door and yanked it open. "Well, when you do come up with an answer, be sure to let me know. I wouldn't want to be kept hanging for a year."

Holly jumped as the door slammed behind him. She stared down at the roses scattered on the floor. How could Stephan do this to her? She'd finally put him in the past and had fallen in love with another man, a man who'd asked her to become a part of his life. And now, she had no choice but to go back to New York and give him an answer she should have given him a year ago. No, she wouldn't marry him! If she were going to marry anyone, it would be Alex Marrin. The only problem was, he hadn't asked.

So why was she determined to return to New York? She didn't have to answer Stephan at all. It had been a year and he'd already found another woman. Her answer should have been obvious. And all she had waiting back in the city was a job she'd grown to hate and a business that barely stayed afloat from year to year.

Holly sighed. Maybe she just needed an excuse, a chance to give herself some time to figure out an answer for Alex. He was the man she really loved, the man she should want to spend her life with. Closing her eyes, she tried to calm the confusion in her mind. She had only dreamed about a future with Alex. And now that her future was close enough to grab, she couldn't reach out and take it, couldn't believe that it might be real.

She flopped back onto the pillows and let images of the previous night drift through her mind. A shiver of desire skittered up her spine as all the feelings they'd shared came rushing back. Intense feelings. Feelings that Holly knew might last a lifetime if she'd only give them a chance. But could she base her whole future on overwhelming passion and desperate love? Or did there have to be more?

HOLLY TOOK A LAST LOOK around the kitchen, a place that had become as familiar as the back of her hand. She'd arranged everything exactly the way she wanted over the past few weeks, utensils in handy spots, staples where she could get at them quickly. This was her kitchen now and she wondered whether it might revert to the mess she'd found it in, like a testosterone jungle swallowing up civilization.

She'd spent her time finishing preparations for the Marrins' Christmas Eve celebration and Christmas dinner, occupying her mind with recipes rather than regrets. ''The

Beef Wellington is kind of tricky,'' she said as Jed listened intently. "I've rolled out the pastry and all you have to do is enclose the filet inside. Work very quickly so that you can get it right into the oven. Otherwise the pastry will get doughy. Then bake thirty to forty minutes. The meat thermometer should read precisely 125 degrees. Watch it carefully.''

She handed Jed the two pages of directions for the Beef Wellington. She wasn't about to tell him that the recipe was straight out of Julia Child—*Filet de Boeuf en Croûte*. He already looked intimidated enough. Holly forced a smile. "Don't worry. This is the most difficult thing. The turkey for tomorrow will be a breeze. You just have to stuff it right before you put it into the oven. The stuffing is in the green bowl.'' She handed him another two pages.

Jed nodded solemnly. "I—I think I can do that.''

She handed him another sheet of paper. "Here are all the directions for all the side dishes. And diagrams of the table settings. Don't forget to change the candles. Red for tonight, white for tomorrow.''

"That's important?'' Jed asked.

"Very,'' Holly said. "I've ironed all the table linens and carefully folded them. The poinsettia print is for tonight, the white cutwork tablecloth is for tomorrow. Come to think of it, I should probably just set the table for tonight and save you the time.'' She turned to hurry to the dining room, but Jed's voice stopped her.

"Couldn't you stay?'' he reminded her. "I've never stuffed a bird before and this Beef Burlington kind of has me flummoxed. I'm not sure I've ever used a meat thermometer before.''

"Wellington. And I—I can't stay. I've got…business back in New York. Something I have to take care of right away.''

"He asked you to stay, didn't he," Jed said.

"I'd really rather not talk about it," Holly said. "I'm a little confused right now and the more I think about it, the more confused I get. My brain is starting to hurt. I—I just need some time. This is a very big decision for me. I don't want to make a mistake."

"Well, he's not doing much better. That boy's cleaned out stalls so good you could eat off the floor. If you had a mind to, that is. There'll be no more Stony Creek pedicures."

Holly had wondered what Alex had been doing for the past twenty-four hours. She hadn't caught a single glimpse of him, not that she'd been looking. He was obviously still angry over her refusal to give him an answer. But no amount of convincing would change her mind. Holly had always taken her time making decisions and planning her future. She wasn't about to uproot herself and move to Schuyler Falls after one night of incredible passion, no matter how wonderful he made her feel or how strongly he professed his love.

She had to consider her options, to carefully contemplate every detail until she knew things would turn out perfect. But was that ever possible? Every couple went into a relationship expecting it to turn out perfect and that didn't always happen. Alex had tried once before and failed. Would they also be a casualty of the odds? Were the odds already stacked against them? Or had fate purposely brought them together?

She sighed. "Well, I think we've covered everything. My bags are by the front door and my train leaves in thirty minutes. We should probably get going." Holly gave Jed an encouraging smile. "Don't worry, you'll do fine. And the Beef Wellington will taste great even if it is a little overcooked and the pastry is doughy." She grabbed her coat from the back of a chair and shrugged into it. "I better say goodbye to Eric. Do you know where he is?"

"He's waiting on the front porch. You make your farewells and I'll get your bags and warm up the truck," Jed said.

Holly nodded, then slowly walked to the front door. She found Eric sitting on the steps, staring out at the snow-covered driveway, Thurston lying next to him in a spot of sunshine. She quietly closed the door behind her then sat down beside him. He didn't look at her and she could see he was close to crying.

Slipping her arm around his shoulders, she pulled him closer and kissed the top of his head. "We've had a good time, haven't we? You got your perfect Christmas, didn't you?"

He nodded. "It would be more perfect if you'd stay," Eric suggested. "I was thinking you could be my mom…if you wanted to." He glanced up at her, his gaze full of hope.

"I don't know what the future holds," Holly said. "Maybe someday, I will be your mom. Or maybe someone wonderful will come along and make you and your dad very happy. But that doesn't mean I'll ever stop loving you."

"Yeah," Eric said. "That's what my mom said when she left."

Holly felt his words stab into her heart, robbing her of her breath. She pushed back her own tears. Why did this sweet child have to suffer for their indecision? Why couldn't they all be a happy family? "Well, just pretend that I'm a real angel. And believe that I'll be watching over you from a long way away."

Eric reached into his pocket and withdrew a crudely wrapped box. "It's a Christmas gift. I bought you bubble bath, but then I decided to give you this instead. You can open it.''

Holly tore the wrapping and picked through the little box lined with cotton. She withdrew a chain. Hanging from it was a penny, shiny and nearly flattened paperthin. ''It's beautiful,'' she said.

''It's my lucky penny. Me and Kenny and Raymond put pennies on the train tracks and when we came back the next day they were squished. I had this penny when I went to see Santa, when I asked him for you. Now, you can have it. For luck.''

Holly slipped the chain around her neck, a tear slipping from the corner of her eye, her heart nearly breaking. ''Thank you, Eric. It's the best present ever.''

He grinned, then stood up and wrapped his arms around her neck. ''It's for the best angel ever.'' He finally let go of her neck, then turned and raced back inside the house, Thurston trotting after him.

Holly drew a deep breath and rose, the penny still clutched between her thumb and index finger. Then she started down the steps. Jed waited for her in the truck, her bags already tucked in the back. She walked slowly, hoping that Alex would magically appear and sweep her into his arms so she couldn't possibly leave. That's what she wanted, wasn't it? She wasn't ready to make a decision, not yet, but she didn't want to leave. With a few hundred miles between them, she was afraid her attraction to Alex would fade a little, the hazy world of passion they'd shared would disappear and she'd never see this place again.

When she reached the truck, she grabbed hold of the door handle, then turned around for one last look. To her surprise, she saw Alex standing by the corner of the porch, his hands hitched on his waist, his hair blown by the crisp wind. Holly felt her breath catch in her throat, exactly the way it had the very first time she'd set eyes on him.

Alex took a single step nearer. "I guess this is goodbye then," he called.

She moved away from the truck. "I suppose it is, at least for the time being."

He stared down at his feet. "Are you going back to him?"

Holly shook her head. "I don't love him. And I'm going to tell him that."

"And after that? Will you come back and give me an answer?" Alex asked.

Holly nodded. "I promise. I will."

Jed beeped the truck horn and Holly jumped. She glanced over her shoulder and he pointed to his watch. Then she turned back to Alex. He was staring at her across the distance between them. Without thinking, she ran to him, then pushed up on her toes and brushed a kiss across his cheek. "Merry Christmas, Alex."

He stared down into her eyes and, for a moment, she considered staying, his gaze a connection that couldn't be broken, a connection she didn't want to break for fear they'd never be able to find it again. But then she slowly backed away and got into the truck.

Holly watched him through the back window of the pickup as they bumped down the long driveway to the road. Just before the house disappeared from view, he raised his hand and waved. Her heart ached and her mind whirled with regret, but she forced herself to turn around and look at the road ahead.

"I will come back," she murmured softly. "I promise." But though she said the words, Holly wasn't sure she meant them. After all, this was just supposed to be a job, a two-week project to put her company back in the black. She was never supposed to fall in love.

9

THE TRAIN RIDE BACK to the city seemed to drag on endlessly for Holly. She tried to be excited about going home,
tried to muster enthusiasm about getting back to the hustle
and bustle of a normal life. But with every mile that
passed, Holly's thoughts roiled with regret and indecision.
For two weeks, she'd lived a different life, quiet and important, filled with people who cared about one another.
What did she have waiting in the city except twinkle lights
and pinecone garland and hand-blown Polish ornaments?
A girl certainly couldn't snuggle up with those late at
night.

As the scenery flew by, she slowly savored the memories of her night with Alex, trying to recall in perfect
detail every moment of every minute, choosing to focus
on the passions rather than the problems afterward. Inter-
spersed with the passion was the laughter, images of Eric
baking cookies and Jed standing behind her, taking notes,
as she cooked. Alex's gentle teasing and stolen kisses.

After living at Stony Creek Farm, her life in the city
appeared banal and bleak. Did she really care whether she
put the finest holly or the freshest mistletoe in her Christmas arrangements? Did she really care whether her ornaments were real mercury glass or just a cheap knockoff?
And if she had to convince one more rich matron that
white twinkle lights weren't the only choice for a Christ-

mas tree, she surely would scream. Holly tipped her head back and sighed.

"The holidays are difficult for everyone, dear."

Holly glanced at the elderly lady sitting next to her. The plump little woman had boarded in Schenectady, and though Holly made it quite clear by her expression that she'd rather sit alone, the lady plopped down beside her. She smelled of lemon verbena and she carried a battered carpetbag that Holly estimated was at least a hundred years old. Her perfume gave Holly a strange sense of déjà vu and then she remembered that her grandmother always used to wear a dab of lemon verbena beneath each ear.

"I'm fine," Holly murmured, turning away to stare out the window. "I'm just tired."

"Are you going to visit relatives? I'm going to see my daughter. She lives in Brooklyn. Perhaps you know her? Selma Goodwin?"

Holly shook her head. "No, I don't know her."

"She leads such an exciting life in the city. Always so busy, working hard, taking care of her family. Sometimes I think she forgets to stop and smell the roses. Do you?"

"Have a family?"

"Smell the roses."

"No," Holly said. "I don't smell the roses." She laughed dryly. "In fact, roses are precisely what got me here in the first place. If it weren't for those damn roses, I'd probably be spending Christmas with Alex and Eric, not sipping low-fat eggnog alone in my apartment. And if Christmas Eve alone isn't pathetic enough, tomorrow I get hit with the double-whammy. Christmas Day *and* my birthday."

"Add a little brandy to that eggnog and you won't feel so bad, dear. Back in my day we didn't use antidepressants when we were blue. We just dipped into the brandy snifter.'' The woman giggled as if she were revealing her darkest secrets, then patted Holly's hand. ''Why don't you tell me all about it? Perhaps I can help.''

All of a sudden, Holly felt the undeniable need to unburden herself. After all, she hadn't been able to make any sense out of the past few weeks. Maybe, looking at the whole situation from an objective point of view, this stranger could. She took a deep breath and went back to the beginning. ''It all started when I got a job as an angel—not a real angel, but a Christmas angel.''

The story poured out of her as the train rumbled through Albany and Hudson, the scenery flying by as she told of her growing feelings for Alex Marrin and his son. The woman didn't say much, but when she did comment, her words were frank and to the point and her questions direct.

''At first we didn't get along,'' Holly admitted, ''but then everything changed between us. Do you believe in love at first sight?''

The woman shrugged. ''I suppose love is love, whether it happens immediately or whether it takes a long time. What I do know about love is that you have to listen to your heart, dear. When I met my Harold, I thought he was the cat's pajamas. But he was all full of himself and didn't even notice me. When he finally did bother to look, he fell hard. I found out later that he ignored me because he was scared of me. Do you believe that? Afraid of me. Deep down inside, I knew he loved me, though.''

''What was he afraid of?''

''I suppose he was afraid that he might not have what it takes to keep me happy. But being with him was all the happiness I needed.'' She sighed. ''Do you love this man?''

''I do,'' Holly said. ''And I know he loves me. But is

that enough? And how do I know that love will last?''
She sighed. ''I just have so many questions and no answers.'' She looked at the older lady bleakly. ''Do you
have any answers for me?''

The train slowly came to a stop, and for the first time,
Holly noticed that they'd pulled into Penn Station, their
ride through the city going completely unnoticed. The
woman stood up and straightened her tidy little suit.
''Only you know how to make your dreams come true,
dear. If you listen to your heart, you'll never go wrong.''
She tucked her carpetbag under her arm. ''Well, dear, it
was a pleasure talking with you. Do have a Merry Christmas, won't you?''

''Wait,'' Holly said. After such intimate conversation,
the woman couldn't just walk away. There was so much
more to discuss! ''I didn't even introduce myself. My
name is Holly. Holly Bennett. What's your name? Maybe
we could catch a cup of coffee.'' Suddenly she didn't
want to go home to her cold, empty apartment. She didn't
even have a Christmas tree of her own.

The woman glanced around and then a smile curved
her lips and she gave Holly a wink. ''Most people call
me Louise. But you can call me…your Christmas angel.''

Then Louise stepped out into the aisle, and before Holly
could even stumble out of her seat, she'd been swallowed
up by the crowd of holiday passengers anxious to get off
the train. Holly dragged her luggage from the overhead
shelf and forced her way into the aisle. ''Wait! Louise! I
wanted to thank you. And tell you that—''

By the time she got off the train, her Christmas angel
had disappeared. Holly lugged her bags down the platform, wishing that she'd had just a few more minutes with
Louise, received a few more bits of sage advice. '''Only
you know how to make your dreams come true,''' Holly

murmured. "I could make my dreams come true right now if I wasn't such a dope. I could listen to my heart and change the course of my life."

Her spirits suddenly lifted and her surroundings brightened. In an instant she was filled with holiday cheer and Holly hurried toward the terminal, weaving through the crush of the crowd. This could be the very best Christmas ever and all she had to do was ignore all the questions in her head and listen to her heart. As she walked through the doors, she glanced around frantically, trying to figure the most direct way to the ticket counter. With all the holiday travellers, she would be lucky to get a ticket. If she couldn't, there was always the bus. Or a rented car. Heck, she'd walk if she had to, but she was going to get back to Schuyler Falls if it was the last thing she did.

"Holly!"

She heard her name above the din of the crowd and she stopped and glanced around. "Louise?"

"Holly, over here. It's me! Meg."

Holly stood on her tiptoes and scanned the crowd, catching sight of Meg's curly red hair about fifteen feet away. She worked against the traffic and it took her nearly a minute to make it to the spot where her friend stood. "Meg, what are you doing here?" she asked breathlessly. "Is everything all right?"

"Not exactly. I called the farm. Alex Marrin told me you'd left on the first train." She shoved her hands into the pockets of her coat and stared at the floor, two spots of color reddening each cheek. Meg wasn't easily rattled and Holly had never seen her look so uneasy.

"What is it?" Holly asked. "Is it Eric?"

Meg shook her head. "I've done something I don't think you're going to like. But I want you to know, I had the very best intentions. I just really didn't expect you to come back. I thought you'd realize you were in love with him and you'd stay. And that would put an end to all your doubts. But my plan kind of backfired.''

Holly frowned. ''Meg, what did you do?''

Meg winced, then shook her head. ''I sent the roses and signed Stephan's name.'' She cover her face with her hands. ''I'm a bad, bad friend. And a terrible business associate. And I wouldn't blame you if you hated me forever and fired me on the spot. I just thought if you were forced to make a choice you'd realize—''

Holly laughed and threw her arms around Meg's neck, stopping her explanation. ''*You* sent the flowers.'' She pressed her palm to her chest. ''Thank God. Do you know what this means?''

''That I'm out of a job?''

Holly hugged her again. ''No! It means I don't have to face Stephan and tell him that I never wanted to marry him. God, I wasn't looking forward to that.''

''Then I still have a job?''

''I could never fire you. Besides, after today, you're the president and sole owner of All The Trimmings. And I'm moving to Schuyler Falls to live with the man I love.''

''What? You're going to marry Alex Marrin?''

''Well, he hasn't asked me yet. But I'm going to do my best to convince him that I'll make a wonderful wife,'' Holly said, grabbing her bags from the floor. ''I should have stayed in the first place, but the train ride gave me a chance to realize how I feel. The farther I traveled from Alex and Eric, the more I ached to see them again. I'm in love with Alex Marrin and I want to have a life with him. He loves me, Meg. And I'm going to buy a ticket back to Schuyler Falls and be a part of his family.''

"How long until the train leaves? I hope it leaves soon. Do you think Holly will be happy when we show up at her house? Can I sit by the window?"

Alex watched through the lightly falling snow as his son paced back and forth across the station platform. He'd tried to convince Eric to wait inside, where it was warmer, but he needed space to move and a chance to burn off a little of his excess energy. They had a long train ride ahead of them and Alex hoped Eric would spend it sleeping, giving him plenty of time to plan a strategy.

It had taken all of two minutes for him to regret letting Holly go that morning. He fingered the ring in his pocket. The truck had barely been out of sight and he was already wondering how he'd be able to get her back. He'd cursed his pride and his cowardice at not asking her to marry him, then tried to come up with a plan to convince her they belonged together for the rest of their lives. Luckily, Eric had forced his hand, taking another jaunt to the train station without his father's permission. So they'd both ended up here at the Schuyler Falls train station, awaiting the next train to New York City.

"How could you let her leave?" Eric asked, sitting down next to him, then immediately standing.

"I was momentarily insane," he said, then leveled his gaze at his son. "Like you were momentarily insane when you hopped the bus and came down here to the station all on your own."

"You found me," Eric said. "Even though I didn't tell you where I was going, you knew where to find me."

"Your little adventures to the train station and Dalton's Department Store are going to stop. Or you'll be grounded until you're eighteen and I'll take away every Game Boy you own and hope to own."

"It's worth it," Eric said. "We're going to get my

Christmas angel back. You can have all my toys. And you can even have the car that Gramps was going to give me when I learn to drive.''

"You want Holly back that bad?"

Eric nodded. "I want her to come and live with us forever. And bake me gingerbread and teach me how to play the piano and tell me how to act around girls."

Alex arched his eyebrow. "Holly talked to you about girls?"

"We talked about everything," Eric said. "She really knows a lot about girls, probably because she is one."

"Yeah, that helps. It's hard to navigate the female mind without a map."

"Yeah," Eric agreed. "And you're not good at it at all, Dad." He sent him a pointed glance, as if he'd suddenly become the parent and Alex was now the child. "You better hope this works. I don't want you to blow it again."

"And what if it doesn't work?" Alex asked. "Eric, you understand that I can't make Holly come back if she doesn't want to. You can't force someone to love you."

"She does love us," Eric said, his tone guileless, yet supremely confident.

"How do you know that? Did she tell you?"

"She didn't have to say it, I just know it. You can tell by the way she looks at you. You know, when you're not looking. She looks all mushy and romantic, like Eleanor Winchell looked when she had a huge crush on Raymond." He raised his voice to imitate his nemesis. "Oh, Raymond, you're so strong. And you're so good at soccer. Can you carry my books? Will you buy me a candy bar?" He scoffed. "Like she needs another candy bar."

Alex jumped in at the first break in Eric's diatribe. "So what did Holly tell you about women? I mean, girls."

"She said that if you treat 'em nice, the good girls, the

ones worth liking, will be nice back. And if they're not, then they're not worth knowing."

"Well, I guess that pretty much sums it up."

Eric sat down next to him and patted Alex's knee. "So, when does the train leave? Is it time yet? Can we get a soda in the dining car?"

Alex sat back on the bench and crossed his legs in front of him. Truth be told, he hadn't been very nice to Holly. He should have told her flat out that he wanted to marry her, that she meant the world to him and he couldn't live without her. He should have pushed aside all his doubts and taken a chance.

"There it is!" Eric shouted, jumping to his feet and pointing down the tracks.

"That's not it, Scout. That train's going the wrong way. That one's coming from New York. Our train doesn't leave for another forty-five minutes."

"How long will it take us to get there?"

"A little over three hours. It'll be very late when we get to Holly's. She might be asleep."

"Will it still be Christmas Eve?" Eric asked.

"Nope, it'll be Christmas Day."

Eric sighed as he sat back down beside Alex. He swung his feet in front of him and hummed a chorus of "Frosty." Alex watched him for a long moment, then fixed his gaze on the approaching train. He'd never done anything like this in his life, taken such a risk with his heart, and he was doing it fully aware of the consequences. But he'd never know unless he tried and the rewards were certainly worth the gamble. He just hoped Eric wouldn't take it too badly if it all fell apart.

The train slowed as it approached the station, the brakes grinding and the engine rumbling. Eric covered his ears and laughed, then jumped up to watch the conductor as he hopped off the train and placed the step at the door to the third car.

Through the lighted windows of the train, Alex could see the holiday travelers crowded into the seats and pushing down the aisle. For a moment, he saw a woman who looked remarkably like Holly. And then she was gone. Alex shook his head. She'd been on his mind all day long, images of her swirling in his head until he knew the only way to stop them would be to see her again.

What would he say? He'd have to start with an apology—first, for waking her, second, for showing up unannounced, and then, probably for everything he'd done wrong in the past two and a half weeks. After that was finished, he'd have to explain how he felt. He'd plead his case, hoping to convince Holly to give up her life in New York for a life as a wife and a mother at Stony Creek Farm. If she insisted on living in the city, he'd have to find a way to keep the farm running until Eric was ready to take over. It wouldn't be easy, but it wouldn't be impossible. And then, there was—

Eric tugged on his jacket sleeve. "Dad! Dad, look!"

"It's not time yet, Scout."

"No, look!" Alex turned and followed Eric's pointed finger, but all he saw were hurrying passengers.

"At what?"

"It's our Christmas angel!" Eric cried.

She materialized out of the crowd as if by magic, the passengers suddenly parting to leave her standing on the platform alone. The light above her head bathed her in luminescent beams, reflecting off the softly falling snow until it looked as if she were showered with tiny diamonds.

Alex slowly rose and took a step toward her, not sure whether she was real or just a dream. Either way, she was

the most beautiful thing he'd ever seen. And if he knew
only one thing, he knew he was looking at his future.

THE PLATFORM WAS CROWDED as Holly descended from
the train, luggage and shopping bags jostling her as passengers passed. Now that she was here, she wasn't certain
what she was supposed to do. Everything had been so
clear, standing in the middle of Penn Station, her return
ticket clutched in her hand. But now that she was back in
Schuyler Falls, her doubts had crept back.

It was just after seven and she imagined that Alex and
Eric and Jed were probably just sitting down to her carefully prepared Beef Wellington. Or maybe they'd gone to
church. "I'll call first," Holly murmured, turning to
search out a pay phone. "Maybe I shouldn't call. What
if he tells me to go back home? What will I do then?"

There had to be cabs waiting in front of the station.
She'd buy a ride to Stony Creek Farm and stand on Alex's
porch once again, praying that he'd let her into his life as
he'd done that first night. He'd said he loved her. If that
was really true then he'd have to be happy to see her
again.

She started toward the doors to the station, but her attention was caught by a tall figure standing at the end of
the platform. Her heart fluttered and her breath caught.
Though she couldn't see his face clearly in the feeble
light, she knew who it was.

He took a step closer and Holly's knees went weak.
She dropped her bags beside her, and though she wanted
to run to him, to throw her arms around him and kiss him,
she suddenly couldn't move.

Alex slowly approached and everything around her, the
train, the passengers, the brightly lit station, faded into the
background. All she could hear was her heart beating in

her chest and all she could see was the man she loved, walking toward her.

When he finally stood in front of her, Eric hovering behind, she reached out to touch him, just to make sure he was real. His jacket was soft, his muscled chest warm beneath the fabric. "You're here. How did you know I was coming back?"

"I didn't." He reached in his pocket and held up a train ticket. "Eric and I were coming to New York to get you."

Tears sprang to the corners of Holly's eyes and ran down her cheeks. She brushed them away with shaking fingers. "You were?"

Alex nodded. "I know I've made a real mess of things, Holly, but I swear, I'm going to make it all up to you. Starting now." From his pocket he withdrew a small velvet bag. "I should have given this to you when I first asked you to stay, but I'm glad I saved it for now, when I can do things right." He took a diamond ring from the little bag and held it up to her. "Holly, I love you. And I'll never stop loving you. Will you marry me?"

"Marry you?"

He nodded. "I never want to let you go again. I want you in my life—and Eric's—forever. Marry me, Holly. Make my life perfect."

Holly watched as he slipped the ring on her finger. The diamond glinted in the glare from the light above her head. "This ring has been worn by three generations of women—my mother, my grandmother and my great-grandmother. All women loved by Marrin men. And I want you to have it."

Tears welled up in her eyes, blurring her vision until the entire scene seemed more like a dream than reality. But it was wonderfully real. And if she'd had any doubts at all, they were gone now, banished to the past, never to be heard from again. The scene was perfect, the three of them standing on a deserted train platform, holiday music crackling from a speaker overhead, and snow falling all around them as the train pulled from the station.

Eric moved to her side and took her hand. ''Please say yes,'' he murmured. ''Please say yes.''

Holly glanced down at Eric and gave his hand a squeeze. ''Yes,'' she murmured. Then she looked into Alex's gaze and nodded. ''Yes, Alex. I will marry you.''

Eric shouted for joy and jumped up and down as Alex pulled her into his arms. He took her face between his hands and kissed her, softly and gently, a kiss filled with love. Then he picked up Eric and gathered them both in his arms. Holly laughed and tipped her face up to the falling snow.

She'd always worked so hard to give other people a perfect Christmas. But now, standing here with Alex and Eric, she realized that a perfect Christmas didn't have anything to do with fancy trees and pretty gifts. A perfect Christmas was about love and happiness, about family and home. And for Holly, this was finally *her* perfect Christmas.

Epilogue

ERIC LAY ON HIS STOMACH in front of the blazing fire in the library. Wads of paper were strewn all around him and his new toys were temporarily forgotten for a much more important matter. They'd just finished a huge turkey dinner, the conversation centering on wedding plans and a honeymoon for three at Disney World.

Eric glanced over his shoulder. Gramps was snoozing in a chair, his third piece of cherry pie half-eaten on the table beside him. Thurston was curled up near the window. And his dad and Holly were snuggled up on the couch, talking in quiet tones and laughing.

They'd spent the night in the barn, watching Jade give birth to a pretty little filly. And this morning at breakfast, after they sang "Happy Birthday," his dad had presented Holly with a special birthday present—Jade's foal. Eric smiled. Now he knew Holly could never leave. She had her own horse at Stony Creek Farm. She'd even given it a name already. Since she'd known the Marrin horses were named after gemstones or flowers, she hadn't pondered it for more than a moment. She'd simply held up her left hand, smiling, and stated, "Diamond."

Eric turned back to the letter. When he'd asked for a Christmas angel, he'd never expected to get a brand-new mom. But he couldn't think of a better Christmas gift than Holly, except for…He clutched his pencil in his hand and carefully considered the text of his letter. This letter had to be perfect—as perfect as the last letter he wrote to Santa. For this time he was asking for something really big! He had almost a year to get the letter just right before he'd deliver it directly to Santa at Dalton's Department Store, a year to work on his penmanship and choose the right envelope.

He stared down at the letter, stumped by the next word. Eric softly sounded it out. "B-R-U—" No, that wasn't right. "How do you spell 'brother?'" he called out.

"Why do you need to know how to spell that?" his dad asked.

He sat up and faced the sofa, deciding whether he should tell Dad and Holly about his newest letter to Santa. Heck, it couldn't hurt. To make this Christmas wish come true he'd need all the help he could get. "I'm writing to Santa and asking him to bring me a baby brother," he replied.

His father gasped and Holly's eyes went wide. "A brother?"

"Yeah. After you and Holly get married, it would be all right, wouldn't it? I'd ask for a real good baby, one that didn't cry and barf all the time."

"We haven't really talked about that," his father said. He turned to Holly. "Have we?"

Holly shrugged. "What about a sister?" she asked.

He watched as they kissed for about the billionth time that day. Eric figured he'd have to get used to all the smooching if Holly was going to marry his dad.

"A girl?" Eric crinkled his nose. "If there are no boys left, I guess a girl would be all right...as long as she doesn't turn out like Eleanor Winchell."

Eric's dad wrapped his arm around Holly's shoulders and drew her near. "I think she'd turn out just like Holly. Pale hair and pretty features and as sweet as sugar."

"Then I'd like her," Eric said.

His father motioned to Eric. "Bring that letter here, Scout," he said. Eric crawled across the room, the paper clutched in his hand. He gave it to his father, then sat back on his heels and watched as he folded it up and handed it to Holly.

"What am I supposed to do with this?" Holly asked.

"File it," Dad said. "For future use."

"Future?" Holly asked.

Eric's father chuckled. "Yeah. We'll work on it later tonight."

Eric grinned, then crawled back to his spot in front of the fireplace. He tore a fresh sheet of paper from his pad and snatched up his pencil. Now that he had the brother taken care of, he could ask Santa for something else. Maybe if he wrote a really good letter, he could get them two babies.

"Yeah," he murmured. "Two babies. Twins—a boy *and* a girl." Now *that* would be a *perfect* Christmas!

Modern Romance™
...seduction and
passion guaranteed

Tender Romance™
...love affairs that
last a lifetime

Sensual Romance™
...sassy, sexy and
seductive

Blaze
...sultry days and
steamy nights

Medical Romance™
...medical drama on
the pulse

Historical Romance™
...rich, vivid and
passionate

27 new titles every month.

*With all kinds of Romance for
every kind of mood...*

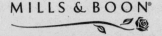

FREE
2 BOOKS
AND A SURPRISE GIFT!

We would like to take this opportunity to thank you for reading this Mills & Boon® book by offering you the chance to take TWO more specially selected titles from the Modern Romance™ series absolutely FREE! We're also making this offer to introduce you to the benefits of the Reader Service™—

- ★ FREE home delivery
- ★ FREE monthly Newsletter
- ★ FREE gifts and competitions
- ★ Exclusive Reader Service discount
- ★ Books available before they're in the shops

Accepting these FREE books and gift places you under no obligation to buy; you may cancel at any time, even after receiving your free shipment. Simply complete your details below and return the entire page to the address below. ***You don't even need a stamp!***

YES! Please send me 2 free Modern Romance™ books and a surprise gift. I understand that unless you hear from me, I will receive 4 superb new titles every month for just £2.55 each, postage and packing free. I am under no obligation to purchase any books and may cancel my subscription at any time. The free books and gift will be mine to keep in any case.

P2ZEC

Ms/Mrs/Miss/Mr ....Initials ....
BLOCK CAPITALS PLEASE

Surname ....

Address ....

....

....Postcode ....

Send this whole page to:
UK: FREEPOST CN81, Croydon, CR9 3WZ
EIRE: PO Box 4546, Kilcock, County Kildare (stamp required)